Their lips were only an inch apart, distracting Cy from his duty to protect her.

All that registered was Kellie's warmth and beauty, seducing him into wanting a taste of her. It was wrong to give in to his desire, but he'd passed a threshold where chemistry had taken over. He could no more stop what was happening than he could prevent himself from being swept into a vortex.

When his mouth closed over hers, he heard a small moan, then she was giving him access as if she couldn't stop herself either. For a minute he forgot everything while the wonder of her response had took hold of. One kiss became another and another until it all merged into a growing need that set them on fire.

He'd never known this kind of ecstasy before. Maybe it was because of the danger surrounding them that the experience of holding and kissing her had surpassed any pleasure he'd known.

Dear Reader,

I love this quote from Leon Metz in the book
Texas Ranger Tales by Mike Cox:

> A mystique hovers over the Texas Rangers, a
> mystique giving them a quality unlike other war-
> riors or lawmen. They are seen at once as brave,
> resourceful, intrepid, and straightforward. They
> have a reputation as men who keep a-coming
> and never back up.

> Because they have always been a team, scant
> Rangers have become household names. Out
> of the thousands who have served, only a few
> have achieved any notable fame. To most peo-
> ple, Rangers are simply obscure men behind
> the badge, men who did their duty, men who
> avoided the limelight.

In *The Texas Ranger's Bride*, I've written about a
fictitious Ranger named Cyril 'Cy' Vance, featured
in my Lone Star Lawmen series. If you, as the
reader, only remember one Texas Ranger by name,
I hope you'll remember Ranger Vance. To me he
represents the finest of his kind, and a great man.
When you've finished the book, check with his wife.
She'll tell you!

Enjoy!

Rebecca Winters

THE
TEXAS RANGER'S
BRIDE

—

REBECCA WINTERS

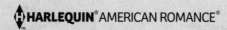
HARLEQUIN® AMERICAN ROMANCE®

Recycling programs
for this product may
not exist in your area.

ISBN-13: 978-0-373-75580-6

The Texas Ranger's Bride

Copyright © 2015 by Rebecca Winters

Printed in U.S.A.

HARLEQUIN®
www.Harlequin.com

Rebecca Winters, whose family of four children has now swelled to include five beautiful grandchildren, lives in Salt Lake City, Utah, in the land of the Rocky Mountains. With canyons and high alpine meadows full of wildflowers, she never runs out of places to explore. They, plus her favorite vacation spots in Europe, often end up as backgrounds for her romance novels, because writing is her passion, along with her family and church.

Rebecca loves to hear from readers. If you wish to email her, please visit her website, cleanromances.com.

Books by Rebecca Winters

Harlequin American Romance

Hitting Rocks Cowboys

In a Cowboy's Arms
A Cowboy's Heart
The New Cowboy
A Montana Cowboy

Daddy Dude Ranch

The Wyoming Cowboy
Home to Wyoming
Her Wyoming Hero

Undercover Heroes

The SEAL's Promise
The Marshal's Prize
The Texas Ranger's Reward

This and other titles by Rebecca Winters are also available in ebook format from Harlequin.com.

Dedicated to Christopher R. Russell,
a military warrior from Texas who has become
a cherished friend. *This is for you, Sarg.*

Chapter One

"This is Tammy White and you're listening to Hill Country Cowboy Radio broadcasting from Bandera, Texas, the Cowboy Capital of the World!

"Oh boy, have we got a lineup for you on this Labor Day weekend, including the star of the Bandera Rodeo, Kellie Parrish from Austin, Texas, our state's hopeful to win the National Barrel Racing Championship in Las Vegas come December. She'll be our guest in the second segment of our show.

"Now hear this. All you cowgirls out there, listen up and hold on to your Stetsons because we have some jaw-dropping, gorgeous, bronco-busting, homegrown cowboys in studio. But that's not the best part. They're four of our famous, legendary Texas Rangers, the pride of the great state of Texas! I've asked my buddy Mel from the fire department to be on hand in case I go into cardiac arrest. It's not every day I'm surrounded by such hunky men. They're not only easy on the eyes, but they wear the star and put their lives on the line every day to protect us.

"Welcome, gentlemen. How come we're so lucky

that four of you were willing to be interviewed? Judging by the way you were laughing when you came into the booth, does it mean you're good friends both on and off duty?"

The men all looked at Cy. Their captain in the Austin office had asked him to be the spokesman for this interview. None of them wanted to do it, but the boss insisted it was important for the Rangers to have a positive public presence. Cy had to cowboy up.

"Yup. The four of us share a very unique bond."

"We want to hear all about it, but first why don't you introduce yourselves and tell us where you're from?"

"Sure. I'm Cyril Vance and call Dripping Springs home." Kit took his turn next. "Ranger Miles Saunders from Marble Falls." Vic followed. "Ranger Stephen Malone. I grew up in Blanco." Cy nodded to Luckey on the other side of Vic. "I'm Ranger James Davis from Austin."

"Ladies, it's too bad this isn't television! You'd eat your hearts out if you were sitting where I am. Through the Hill Country grapevine the station learned that a lot of Rangers are in Bandera to help celebrate Jack Hays Days. You'll see them riding their horses in tomorrow morning's parade. It would be hard to believe that anyone in the state of Texas doesn't know the name Jack Hays. But just in case you don't, we want to hear from you why the name of Jack Hays stirs the hearts of every Texan, particularly those of the Rangers."

"I'll take this," Vic volunteered. "When Sam Houston was reelected to the presidency in December 1841, he recognized the effectiveness of the Rangers. And on

January 29, 1842, he approved a law that officially provided for a company of mounted men to 'act as Rangers.' As a result, 150 Rangers under Captain John Coffee 'Jack' Hays were assigned to protect the southern and western portions of the Texas frontier. Houston's foresight in this decision proved successful in helping to repel the Mexican invasions of 1842, as well as shielding the white settlers against Indian attacks over the next three years."

Vic turned to Kit. "You tell the rest."

"Be happy to. Jack Hays was responsible for improving the quality of recruitments and initiating tough training programs for the new Rangers, as well as initiating an esprit de corps within his command.

"The Paterson Colt six-shooters had just been invented and Captain Hays and his men were fortunate to be armed with these weapons instead of single shotguns. When the Comanche attacked Captain Hays and his company of forty in Bandera Pass in 1842, they were defeated."

"Gentlemen? I found a quote from Walter Prescott Webb, a twentieth-century US historian who said, 'Their enemies were pretty good…the Texas Rangers had to be better.' Do you Rangers still use those old six-shooters? If not, what kind of weapons do you carry?"

Luckey spoke up. "We use a variety that includes the .357-caliber SIG Sauer, the .45-caliber Colt automatic, the SIG Sauer P226 pistol, the Ruger mini-14 automatic rifle and the Remington 12-gauge shotgun."

"There are dozens of questions I want to ask, but

since you're pressed for time, why don't you tell our listeners why the four of you are particularly close?"

Cy nodded. "When I joined the Rangers, I didn't know any of the men in the company. On my application, I'd mentioned that I was a descendant of one of the men in Captain Jack Hays's company of forty. During my interview with our captain at company H, he told me there were three other Rangers in our company who could also trace their ancestry back to the original company of forty."

"Wow!"

"Wow is right. He got the four of us together. The rest was history."

"Imagine that. What a remarkable coincidence! You guys are the real thing. It's in your genes. Kind of gives you gooseflesh."

Kit chuckled. "That's one way of putting it. I can't remember a time when I didn't want to be a Texas Ranger. The pride my family felt for our heritage was instilled in me."

"It looks like none of you could escape your destiny."

Luckey grinned. "We wouldn't want to."

"I heard a rumor that everyone at Ranger headquarters has nicknamed you four 'the Sons of the Forty.' That's heady stuff."

"We don't mind," Vic stated. "But it gives us a lot to live up to."

"I'd say you're doing a spectacular job. According to your captain, the governor of our state gave you citations six months ago for your capture of a drug cartel ring on the most-wanted list. Do the four of you always work together on a case?"

Cy shook his head. "No. It's a very rare occurrence that we have an opportunity to do something big together, but we help each other out from time to time. Each case is different."

"Cowboys and cowgirls? Our station is honored that these Texan heroes have taken time out of their busy lives to let us know a little bit more about them. I have it on good report from your captain that the Sons of the Forty will be leading other Rangers on horseback from all over the state in the parade tomorrow. That will be the chance for you ladies to feast your eyes on the best of the best! Thank you for coming in. It's been a Hill Country thrill for me and everyone listening."

"Thank *you*," they said in a collective voice.

KELLIE GOT OUT of her truck in front of the radio station, pressed for time. She'd just driven in from Amarillo over three hundred miles away, where she'd made a decent time in the rodeo the night before. But it wasn't the low score she'd wanted. The fact that she didn't get the best time had little to do with her skill or her horse's.

Since she'd been on a five-state, pro rodeo racing circuit over the past five weeks, she'd been deeply unsettled by a guy who'd been following her from venue to venue among Montana, Oregon, Utah, New Mexico and Texas.

He'd come up to her after her win in Pendleton, Oregon, and asked her out on a date. She told him she was married in order to put him off. When she drove to Utah for the Eagle Mountain Rodeo, there he was again while she was brushing down her horse after her event. He was hoping she'd changed her mind and would go out with him.

She warned him that if he ever came near her again, she'd call the police. At the same time she signaled to her horse handler, Cody. He walked over to find out what was wrong and the stalker took off.

Cody was taking care of her horse Starburst, the one she'd brought on this circuit along with her champion palomino, Trixie, who was the best horse Kellie had ever owned. Trixie had helped her get to the Pro National Rodeo Finals, which were held in December. It was only three months away and she didn't need any kind of problems that would cause her to lose focus.

The stalker had so frightened her, she'd stuck with her rodeo buddies for the rest of the night. Later on in Albuquerque, New Mexico, she found a note on her truck window that said she couldn't avoid him forever and accused her of lying about being married. That told her this man had mental problems, and that put her on edge. She kept the note to show the police.

Afraid this wacko might turn up in Amarillo, she'd bunked with her good friend Sally, who was married to Manny Florez, one of the bull riders in the rodeo. Cody stayed with her horses and looked after them.

After one more rodeo tomorrow night in Bandera, she would drive straight to her parents' ranch in Austin instead of going home to her town house. Together they'd go to the police. But right now she needed to get through this radio show and then put her horse through some exercises.

She'd left the animal in the horse trailer at the RV park on the outskirts of town with Sally and her husband. For the time being they were her protection.

Trying to conquer her fear of the man stalking her, she headed toward the entrance of the radio station and collided with the first of a group of tall, jean-clad men in Stetsons and cowboy boots coming out the door.

"Oh—I'm sorry." She stepped back, shocked by a dart of male awareness that passed through her at the contact. "I didn't see where I was going."

"No problem, Ms. Parrish." His eyes were a piercing midnight blue. "Good luck at the rodeo tomorrow evening. We'll be rooting for you." He tipped his white hat to her.

"Thank you," she murmured as they headed to a van in the parking area.

Kellie had met hundreds of cowboys in all shapes and sizes over her years pursuing her dream to get to the Finals. She'd dated quite a few, nothing serious. But these four were exceptionally good-looking. The man she'd brushed against had momentarily caused the breath to freeze in her lungs. Why hadn't *he* been the one to ask her out on a date in Oregon? She might have been a fool and said yes without knowing anything about him.

Stunned by her immediate attraction, she hurried inside the building afraid she was late. The receptionist told her to walk straight back to the broadcast booth.

"Oh, good. I'm glad you're here. We're on a station break. I'm Tammy White. You're even more beautiful in person. Thanks for doing the show. You're one of our state's biggest celebrities."

"Maybe with a few rodeo fans."

"You're too modest. Your appearance here is making my day."

"Thanks, Tammy." Kellie shook hands with her and sat down. "I barely got here in time."

"I don't suppose you bumped into the Sons of the Forty while you were on your way in here?"

Kellie blinked. "I actually did bump into one of them. Wait—aren't they the Texas Rangers who brought down a drug cartel recently? It was all over the news."

"Yup. You had the luck of getting to see them up close and personal." *Up close and personal is right.* "I swear if I weren't married..." Kellie knew exactly what she meant. The man with the deep blue eyes was a Texas Ranger!

Kellie couldn't believe it, except that she could. With his rock-hard physique and rugged features, he looked as if he could handle anything. Come to think of it, he had been wearing a badge over his Western shirt pocket. But she'd been so mesmerized by his male charisma, nothing much else registered.

"Okay, Kellie. We'll be live in seven seconds. Ready?"

"No. I'm no good behind a microphone." Her mind was still on the striking Ranger. Her body hadn't stopped tingling with sensation.

"Don't worry. Leave it all to me. This is going to be fun."

It would be fun if it weren't for the menace lurking

somewhere out there. Thank heaven for Sally and her husband, who were letting her stay in their trailer with them tonight and tomorrow night. Monday morning she'd take off at dawn.

She couldn't get back home fast enough to tell her parents what had been happening and go to the police. Kellie had put off telling them about this, hoping the man would give it up, because she didn't want her folks worrying about her. But she'd gotten a call in the middle of the night last night, which was the last straw. Her stalker was potentially dangerous, and that terrified her.

Cy's captain, TJ Horton, walked into his office Monday morning. The veteran Ranger now sported a head of gray hair, but he still looked tough enough to take on any fugitive and win. "It's good you're back."

"I'm just finishing up some paperwork on my last case."

"I've got a new one I'd like you to look over. It just came up. Come on into my office."

"Sure." He followed him down the hall. The captain told him to shut the door and take a seat. Cy could tell something was up.

TJ sat back in his swivel chair with his hands behind his head and smiled at him. "You men did the department proud over the weekend. I listened to your contribution on Hill Country Cowboy Radio. Whether you liked it or not—" nope, none of them liked it "—she made you guys out as the poster boys of the department. You're now known as the Famous Four. I thought that might happen, but good publicity never hurts in an age when law enforcement takes a lot of unfair hits. The favor you did for me personally was much appreciated."

"Anything to help, sir."

"I heard a *but* in there. Next year I'll pick another bunch to carry the flag."

"That's a relief."

TJ chuckled, but then leaned forward with a serious expression. "The police turned over a case to our office this morning. It's high profile and the victim could be in serious danger. Because the case has crossed state lines, they feel our department is better equipped to deal with it. I'd like your take on this one." He handed him a folder.

Cy nodded and opened it. The name Kellie Parrish leaped out at him. *She* was the person in danger?

With her silvery-gold hair and cornflower-blue eyes, the barrel racer was a knockout. Under other circumstances he would have liked to hang around the radio station and listen to her interview. She'd been on his mind ever since he'd seen her a few days ago.

He scanned the folder's contents. She was being pursued by a stalker. He'd followed Ms. Parrish across her latest five-state racing schedule. She'd given the lieutenant a description of the man and a typewritten note he'd left on her truck windshield.

The most alarming aspect of the case was the fact that this stalker had phoned her cell phone as recently as the middle of Friday night. She'd been asleep in her friend's trailer in Bandera before driving to Austin this morning. Terrified, she'd gathered her parents and come straight to police headquarters.

Cy let out a low whistle. "I met her coming in the radio station as we were leaving on Friday. We watched her perform at the rodeo Saturday night. She had the second-best time."

"That's not only an amazing coincidence, but fortuitous. It isn't often you already have prior knowledge of the victim, so you understand what kind of threat she's been living with."

Especially when he'd found her incredibly attractive.

The hairs lifted on the back of his neck. Cy couldn't remember the last time he'd had this strong a feeling for a woman in passing. Because of the stress of the job, he didn't have much time for dating and hadn't been out with anyone for at least four months. After watching Ms. Parrish's performance at the rodeo, he'd admired her skill and found himself wondering how to go about getting to know her better. Not in his wildest dreams had he thought it would happen like this.

TJ kept on talking. "The police chief told me her parents met her at the station. They're well-heeled ranchers from southeast Austin who are demanding protection for their daughter and are willing to pay for it. Ms. Parrish is a prominent athlete. I've already ruled out a possible kidnapping scheme with a plan to collect a ransom or she would likely have been abducted at her first stop in Montana. Her parents want her to quit the rodeo circuit and stay with them until this lowlife is caught. She's their only child."

Cy got it. Ms. Parrish was their precious baby.

He shifted his attention from the file to his boss. "If you could have seen the way she rides, you'd know she would never agree to that." Even under so much stress, she'd put in a terrific time at the Bandera Rodeo. "Otherwise, I'm certain she would have quit the circuit in Pendleton when he first showed up and returned to Austin to contact the police. Several of her competitors headed for the championship in Las Vegas were also in Bandera competing. My bet is on her winning the whole thing."

TJ shook his head. "In order for that to happen, she would need full-time bodyguards on the circuit with her. Her parents can afford it. I'll call them now and ask them to bring her back to headquarters so you can talk to her. When you've got a feel for what you're dealing with, let me know how you want to handle this case."

"TJ? Send her in to me first. Then I'll talk to her folks." Parents had their own ideas about what should be done. It simplified things to talk to the victim without anyone else in the room. "I'll let you know when I want them to join us."

His boss nodded in understanding.

"Until they arrive I'll dig up some more background information on her. I'd better get to it." Cy got to his feet and headed for his own office. He'd start with the personal information listed on her website and go from there. Uncanny how he'd already planned to look at her site when he got the chance, just to learn more about her.

"Let's see what turns up on you, Ms. Parrish."

He typed it in and sat back. Seconds later, there she was astride her palomino, lying low over her horse as it was racing straight down the alley. Pure poetry.

Kellie Parrish
Born: Austin, Texas, on February 14, 1990
Residence: Austin, Texas
Dad: Bronco Parrish—3-time NFR Bull Rider Champion
Mom: Nadine Parrish—Barrel Racer Finals 4 times
Horses: Smokey, Walnut, Miss Pandora, Crackers, Farley,
Starburst, Trixie
Joined Pro Rodeo at age 11
Total Earnings: $2,103,775
Wrangler NFR Qualification: 10
College National Finals Qualification: 2
National High School Rodeo Finals Qualifications: 4
Pro Wrangler Finals winner, Oklahoma City, OK: 3
Women's Pro Rodeo Association member

Cy read her blog, keeping track of the dates of the
entries for July and August. She'd archived her previ-
ous blogs. Her ardent fans wanted to know all about
her. How come she wasn't married yet? Did she have
a boyfriend?

She'd answered that she preferred to keep her private life private, but she was friendly and encourag-
ing to those trying to become barrel racers themselves.
She urged them to click to her online clinic for point-
ers. That woman was so busy, Cy didn't know how she
had time to breathe.

She'd put her rodeo schedule for the season on a separate page. There were links to the WPR Association
and all the social media accounts. In other words, her
life was pretty well an open book and prime fodder for

the degenerate who'd targeted her. Talk about a sitting duck! A gorgeous one.

His eyes went back to her personal stats. The questions some of the commentors asked about her personal life had grabbed his attention. Some of them might have been sent by the stalker. An idea on how to handle this case had started to form in his mind. He reached for the phone to arrange for their department's sketch artist to be on hand when she came in. They needed a picture to run through the criminal database, which could access the files from every state in the union to come up with a match.

There was no telling how long the creep had been stalking other women or when his sick fantasy about Ms. Parrish had started. She'd been traveling the circuit for a number of years. He could have seen her anywhere at any time. But he'd approached her for the first time in Oregon only four weeks ago. Cy would start there.

In case this man was a serial stalker or worse, he wanted a list of every known stalking incident in the Pendleton area in the past year. While he waited for the Parrish family to arrive at headquarters, he put through a call to the Pendleton police department. He asked them to fax him the names of stalking victims and their descriptions of the men menacing them, whether their cases had been solved or were still open. One of those descriptions might match up with the man Kellie Parrish had described.

Restless, Cy went to the cubbyhole down the hall they called a lunchroom and poured himself a cup of coffee while he waited. He had dozens of questions to ask. Vic walked in on him. Their eyes met.

"Guess who's in the boss's office."

His pulse raced for no good reason. *She's here.* Kellie Parrish had made an impact on all the guys. "I already know. A stalker's after her."

His friend's black brows shot up. "You got the case?" Cy smiled. "How come that never happens to me?" Vic poured himself some coffee. "If you need help…"

"Thanks. I'll let you know." Cy took his mug back to his office.

Before long, TJ appeared at the door with her. She was probably five foot seven without her cowboy boots. "I believe you two have already met. Ms. Parrish? Meet one of our agents, Cyril Vance."

Cy got to his feet and shook her hand. "It's a pleasure to meet you again, Ms. Parrish, even if it is under harrowing circumstances."

Fear had darkened the blue of her eyes. "I hope you forgive me for bumping into one of the Sons of the Forty. I'm the one who's honored." TJ had disappeared.

"Please sit down."

"Thank you." She'd dressed in jeans and a creamy-colored Western shirt. Beneath the overhead light, her neck-length wavy hair had that silvery-gold metallic sheen he found stunning. So were her face and the rest of her curvaceous figure. Absolutely stunning.

"Can I get you coffee or a soft drink?"

"Neither, thanks."

"I'm going to record our conversation if that's all right with you."

"Of course."

"I have the notes taken by the police. It says here this stalker last contacted you by phoning in the middle of the night."

"Yes. That was Friday," she said, tight-lipped. "I don't know how he knew my cell number."

"How many people have you given it to?"

"My parents, closest friends, my cousin Heidi and of course my horse handler, Cody."

"Tell me about him."

"He's been my closest horse friend since middle school. We've both had our dreams. I was going to win the PRO Finals Rodeo this year and teach barrel racing. He was going to help me and then run a stud farm. Cody is engaged and plans to get married after Finals."

He nodded. "When you fill out forms of any kind, do you list it as your contact number?"

"No. It's not written anywhere. I always give out my parents' number. No…wait. I did give my cell phone number to a friend, Olivia Brown, who works at the Women's Pro Rodeo Association in Colorado Springs, Colorado. She used to ride with our Blue Bonnet Posse, but her husband was transferred to Colorado Springs, so she got a job with the rodeo association there."

"I'll want to talk to her. Now I'll need a list of your friends and cousin, and their phone numbers. Here's some paper."

"All right." She got right to work. When she'd finished, she looked up.

He took the list from her. "Thank you. What did the stalker say on the phone?"

She bit her lip. "'You lied about having a husband. Don't you know it's not nice to lie?' Then he hung up."

"Was there just the one call that night?" She nodded. "Now let's talk about everything that happened the first time this man made contact with you."

She shuddered visibly. "It was right after the barrel-racing event and awards. I was in the process of removing the saddle from Trixie when I heard an unfamiliar male voice from behind call me by my first name. I turned around to discover a total stranger invading my space. A lot of guys have approached me over the years wanting a date, so it wasn't unusual."

Cy could believe it.

"I don't mean to sound full of myself. It's just part of what goes on during the racing circuit, and I've always taken it in good fun before turning them down. But this was different. He came too close. After telling him no, he just stood there with a smile that made my stomach churn. Something about him wasn't right."

"Could you tell if he'd been drinking?"

"No. I couldn't smell alcohol. I was holding the saddle in front of me with both hands and I told him I was married, hoping he'd get the message and go away. When he calmly told me to prove it, I would have thrown the saddle at him and called security, but a couple of friends happened to walk over and he disappeared. I didn't see him again until I drove to Utah for the next rodeo at Eagle Mountain a week later."

"You drive a truck and horse trailer?"

"Yes. I live in the trailer while I'm on the road. My

horse handler drives his own truck and trailer carrying one of my other horses."

"Do you own a car?"

She nodded. "A four-door white Toyota sedan. I keep it at the condo when I'm gone."

"Do you own or rent?"

"Rent. After I leave the rodeo circuit, I'll be buying my own place."

"Where's the parking?"

"The double-car garage is in back, but there's parking in front."

"Is it in a complex?"

"It's a two-story town house with neighbors on either side of me."

Cy paused long enough to buzz the artist to come to his office, and then he turned to her. "We need a picture of this man. Without a photograph we'll have to rely on your eyes. Our department artist has a singular gift."

She clasped her hands together. "All right."

"While we wait for him, I want you to think back. Before Pendleton, have you ever had the slightest suspicion that someone had targeted you?"

"No. Never."

That sounded final. Jim showed up at the door with a sketch pad and electric eraser pencil. "Come on in, Jim. Ms. Parrish, our state's reigning barrel-racing champion, is being stalked. Let's see what you can work up."

"Sure." He sat in the chair next to Kellie, eyeing her in male appreciation. "It's a privilege to meet you, Ms. Parrish. We'll start with a sketch. I could use the computer, but a sketch can tell you things the computer can't. Don't get nervous or frustrated. You may think this won't work, but in three out of ten cases a culprit has been caught through a sketch. I'll work from the eyes on out. Shall we get started?"

She nodded and answered one question after another while he sketched. They worked together while he refined his drawing.

Cy asked her for a more thorough description while Jim was working.

"He looks like the guy next door. You know, someone's brother. Maybe late twenties. Kind of lean. Okay-looking. Nutty-brown hair that curls. Short-cropped. Maybe five-ten, but he was wearing cowboy boots. Weighs probably 150 to 160 pounds. Brown eyes. He wore jeans and a different pullover the second time I saw him."

Jim kept working at the sketch and showed her what he'd done. She said, "His nose was a little thinner." After fixing it he asked her to take another look. "What do you think?"

"You truly do have a gift. It's remarkably accurate."

"We try."

Cy took the drawing from him. The guy bore a superficial resemblance to Ted Bundy, the serial killer from several decades back, but he kept the observation to himself. "That's great work, Jim. We'll go with this to put in the Integrated Automated Fingerprint Identification System. Thank you."

"You're welcome." He turned to Kellie. "All bets are on you winning the championship in December."

"Thank you so much."

"If anyone can catch him, Ranger Vance can. See you, Cy."

When Jim left the office, she looked at Cy. "You're called Cy?"

"Short for Cyril." *Don't get sidetracked.* "Your next rodeo is in South Dakota in two weeks, but I understand your parents want you to quit the circuit."

"Yes, but since we talked with the police, Dad has told me he'll hire some bodyguards for me so I can continue to compete."

Cy shook his head. "That won't work. We want to draw out this stalker and arrest him. He'll know if you have people protecting you. That will change the way he has to operate. It will hinder our efforts and prolong the time you're forced to live in terror."

Her eyes clouded. "I don't want to give up competition, not when I'm so close to the Finals in December. Isn't there another way?"

Yes, but he didn't know if she'd consider it. He knew her parents would raise objections.

"There's always another way. If you'll excuse me for a moment, I'll be right back." He left the office and headed for TJ's, knocking on the open door.

His boss's head lifted. "Come on in."

Cy shut the door and sat down. "Where are her parents?"

"In the reception area. Have you got an angle on this case yet?"

He nodded and brought him up-to-date. Then he told him his idea. TJ didn't say anything at first. That didn't surprise Cy. "I know it's unconventional."

"Unconventional? Hell, Cy. It's unorthodox and unheard-of in this department."

"But it could work. This way she could continue winning rodeos."

Another few minutes passed before TJ said, "I'll admit it's brilliant. You realize the two of you will be walking a very thin line."

Yup. Cy knew exactly what he meant and he wasn't talking about the culprit. "I'll need another Ranger working with me. Whoever you can spare."

His eyes squinted. "You think she'll agree?"

"Probably not, but it's worth finding out. She's had the world championship in her sights since she was eleven years old. If she says no, then I'll know I was wrong to think she'd do anything to achieve her goal."

He nodded slowly. "All right. You bring her in here and I'll send for her parents. She doesn't need their permission, but they'll have to be in on this from the start or it won't work. I'll make sure all three of them are fingerprinted before they leave the building today."

"Right."

Chapter Two

Cy's plan was bold. But no matter how many ways he could think of to attack the problem, he kept coming back to his first idea.

"Ms. Parrish?" he spoke to her from the doorway. She got to her feet. "If you'll come with me, we're going to meet in the captain's office with your folks."

They walked down the hall, where Cy met Kellie's parents. She took after her father in height and coloring. From her mother she'd inherited her good looks and figure. He shook their hands.

TJ invited everyone to sit down. "Ranger Vance has looked at every aspect of this case and has come up with a strategy. Every so often our Rangers plan a sting and go undercover. It's a very effective way to flush out a criminal. Your daughter's case presents a challenge because no one wants to see her quit the barrel-racing circuit when she's so close to winning the championship in Las Vegas." He glanced at Cy. "Tell them your thinking."

Cy got to his feet. "You could hire bodyguards. But it would probably cause the culprit to stay away for a time, not *go* away. We want this stalker to be put away permanently, and ASAP. The best thing to do is flush him out."

"That makes sense to me," her father said.

"What if he's followed me here to this office?" Kellie sounded anxious, but was still keeping her composure. Cy admired her for that.

"I'm sure he's done that and a lot of other things. He knows where you and your parents live. He knows your rodeo schedule, your phone number. He knows your routine and enjoys frightening you. But we're going to turn the tables on him and produce the husband he doesn't believe exists."

Those blue eyes rounded in shock.

"A husband is different from a bodyguard who goes with you everywhere. A husband and wife have their moments of separation. While I'm not with you, one of my team will be guarding you from a distance.

"To set this up, you'll announce your secret through your blog. I've read through it. Your fans have pressed you over and over again to reveal if there's a special man in your life. After telling them all this time that your life is private, you're going to tell them that you recently married a cowboy. Furthermore you are looking forward to a long honeymoon after the Finals in Las Vegas.

"By putting the announcement out on the internet, it will prove to the world you are telling the truth. Of course, this stalker still won't believe you because you've been his fantasy for a long time and he doesn't live in anyone's reality but his own. I still have yet to discover if he's a psychotic who has lost all connection to his world, or a psychopath with a serious mental disorder. But in either case he'll be enraged when he reads your blog.

"I can assure you he's been reading it for as long as he's been stalking you, and so far there's been no mention of a husband. He thinks he's safe. I have no doubt that some of the people making comments about your personal life on your blog have come from this lowlife."

At that observation she paled.

"It will torture him that you really could be married. He thinks he knows everything about you and won't be able to stand the fact that he could be wrong. That will bring him out of lurk mode. When he does that, it will be his big mistake.

"We have no idea of his place of birth or where he lives. He could be from Austin and followed you all the way to Oregon to begin his reign of terror. You can be sure he has already cased your condo and your parents' ranch and knows every move you make. The Pendleton police are sending me a list of stalking victims in the Pendleton area in case there's a way to link him to your case.

"If he'd wanted to kidnap you to compel your parents to pay a ransom, it would have already happened. So we can conclude money is not his motive. Though you didn't see him in Albuquerque, we know he was out there somewhere putting a note on your windshield and phoning you in the middle of the night in Bandera. According to your schedule, you have another rodeo in South Dakota in two weeks. For the time being I imagine you'll be training here in Austin every day until you leave. He's probably planning to do something to you while you're not on the road. Remember—he feels invincible."

When she heard Cy's assessment of the situation, he noticed she'd lowered her head, causing the strands of her molten hair to catch the light from overhead.

"So far you've had your handler and other people around while you've been taking care of your horses. But he'll assume you'll be alone in your condo part of the time for the next two weeks. The beauty of this plan is that when he comes after you, I'll be there watching for him. When he makes his move, he'll discover your husband on the premises. Do you have any questions?"

Now was the time for Kellie to tell him she couldn't go along with his plan. He held his breath, waiting for her parents to voice their objections. Instead, her mother looked at her daughter with an anxious expression.

"His plan sounds solid, but how do you feel about it, honey?"

He watched Kellie nervously moisten her lips. "I'm thankful I won't have to be alone." She looked up at Cy. "Even if it means everyone will think I'm married, I want that disgusting creature caught." Her voice shook.

TJ sent Cy a silent message. *I'll be damned.*

"Before you go home with your parents, I'll need your key to the condo and your phone, Ms. Parrish."

"All right." Her hands trembled as she rummaged in her purse for those items and handed them to him.

"What's the code to get into the garage?" She told him. "Keep your mailbox key."

"Oh. Okay."

He looked at his watch. "Give me six hours, then all of you come to the condo with any luggage you took on the road and I'll let you in. Pick up your mail on the way in, but don't go through it. Act as normally as you can. We'll talk details inside your condo so we're all tuned in to the same channel."

Kellie's father shook Cy's hand again. "Our daughter didn't tell us what had been happening to her until this morning. It's a nightmarish situation and we're very grateful that you're willing to take her case. We'll all be praying this plan works."

"Thank you for helping her," Kellie's mother said with tears in her eyes.

"It's our job and I'm happy to do it. I'll see you later."

He watched Kellie walk out with them. Cy knew in his gut that this stalker didn't want money. He wanted to do her harm. She'd said he looked as if he was in his late twenties. He wondered how many women before Kellie had already been terrorized by him. The stalker fit the general profile for a predator who was usually from eighteen to thirty.

After they left TJ's office, Cy turned to his boss. "Her condo is in West Austin. I'm going to need help to set things up before they arrive."

"This is a high-priority case. Vic just finished a case and is in the building right now. I'll ask him to assist you before assigning him a new case."

Nothing could have pleased him more. "Thanks, TJ." There wasn't a lot of time. They'd have to assemble a team fast.

Not long after he'd returned to his office to send the artist's sketch to the database, Vic walked in. "I'm all yours." He planted himself on a corner of the desk. "That stint on the radio must have put the boss in a good mood."

"It was so important to him, he actually went along with my plan."

"Which is?"

"Outrageous, but Ms. Parrish agreed to it, too, rather than leave the circuit. She wants to win that championship. I figured she would put her desire to achieve her lifelong goal over her fear of this stalker. We're going to pretend to be married so I can protect her day and night."

"What?" Vic's black eyes narrowed. He got to his feet. "You're kidding me."

Cy gave his friend a sharp look. "Can you think of a better way to get the job done?"

They'd known each other a long time. "Hell, no. It's genius, but—"

"But it doesn't hurt that she's a beautiful woman, right?" He couldn't help but read his friend's mind. "I've examined my motives and have decided that even if she were someone else, it wouldn't make a difference. She's been working her whole life to achieve her goal. For her to quit now would be the end of her dreams, not only for this year, but maybe forever. Anyone with her kind of skill and drive deserves all the help she can get."

"I agree with you."

"This guy is a creep who's been tormenting her for a month. She told him she was married so he'd leave her alone. All that did was fan the flames, so I've decided it's time she produced a husband. I want to catch this stalker, Vic, and believe this is the best way to capture his attention and nab him."

"Where do you want to start?"

"We'll get a surveillance team set up in the van to monitor her when I can't be with her." Cy handed him the sketch.

Vic studied it for a minute. "You know who he looks like?"

"Yup, but let's not go there. In case he's camped out by her condo, you and I will impersonate roofers so we can get in around the back of the building through her garage without him suspecting anything. I want to lift any fingerprints we can find. We'll rig the interior with a camera. Let's move."

He folded her list of names and numbers and put it into his pocket. The note she'd given the police needed to go down to the lab. He already had a list a mile long of things to be done before she arrived with her parents. They'd need wedding rings.

KELLIE CHECKED HER watch as her father drove them to the front of her condo in her parents' Volvo sedan. Six thirty p.m. She still couldn't believe what she'd agreed to. She and the striking Texas Ranger had to pretend to be married starting tonight!

What have I done? She closed her eyes. *You've done what's necessary to survive.*

"Come on, honey. Let's go in and have dinner. You haven't eaten all day."

"I couldn't." But her parents had insisted on picking up some barbecue for all of them.

She hadn't had an appetite since this first started. As for sleep… Nothing seemed real. That monster could have been following them from the ranch. She almost expected him to suddenly appear at the mailbox.

The normal number of bills had stacked up. She put the mail into her purse before getting back in the car. Her mom had been over to her condo several times this past month to water her plants and make sure everything was all right. Thank goodness the Ranger would find her house clean and in good shape. There were times when it looked a mess.

She eyed the condo. No one would know the secret it was holding. If everything had gone as planned, then the Ranger was inside. A vision of the way he'd looked when she'd bumped into him in Bandera was indelibly impressed in her mind. He was a man whose aura gave the impression he could deal with anything or one. Her pulse raced at the realization they would be spending time together.

Kellie got out of the car and hurried up the front steps ahead of her parents. He must have heard them because he opened the door to let them in.

"Hi." His deep voice filtered through to her insides.

Kellie looked up at him. "Hi." He'd changed into a dark blue sport shirt and jeans. His eyes matched his shirt. Outside the radio station, he'd been wearing his white Stetson. But in his office as well as now, the light in the living room illuminated the sun-bleached tips of his wavy light brown hair.

Her mother was carrying the food. "I've brought dinner for all of us."

The Ranger smiled and took the bag from her. "Thank you, Mrs. Parrish. How did you know I'm starving?"

The way the corners of his eyes crinkled sent a surprising curl of warmth through Kellie, who put her purse on a chair. While he and her mother went to the kitchen, she turned to help her father carry her bags upstairs to the bedroom. That was when she saw that another couch had been added to the living room. Everything had been rearranged so it would fit.

As they passed the guest bedroom upstairs, she saw some of the Ranger's things on the bed. She avoided her father's eyes and continued to her room.

"Are you okay, Kellie?"

"I don't know what I am yet, but knowing this Ranger is here to protect me is all that's helping keep my sanity right now."

Her dad gave her a big hug. "I'm relieved, too. The captain told me Ranger Vance was one of the men who brought down the drug cartel earlier in the year. He says there's no one better, and I believe him. Come on. Let's go back down and hear what this Ranger has to say."

Kellie nodded. "I'll be there in a minute." She needed to pull herself together.

He kissed her forehead and left. She took time to freshen up in the bathroom before joining everyone at the dining room table. When the Ranger saw her, he stood. "I'm sure it's strange for you to feel like a guest in your own home."

"I'm too thankful you're here to think about it."

He sat back down. "These ribs are delicious. Thank you. I work better on a full stomach. Tonight I'm going to help your daughter draft her marriage announcement message for her blog. By ten it will be out on the internet. As her parents, you'll be bombarded with questions from everyone who knows you. I want you to tell them that Kellie and I met on the circuit. It was love at first sight and we couldn't stand to wait, so we were privately married before her rodeo performance in Montana.

"Tell people there will be a wedding reception for us at the ranch in December, after Finals. Don't say any more or any less. We'll worry about explanations after this stalker is caught."

This is really happening. She eyed her parents, who agreed to do exactly as he said. He had a way of instilling confidence and trust.

He looked at them. "From here on out, Kellie is going to do what she would do if there were no threat. The three of you will carry on with your lives while I work behind the scenes. No one is to know about this case except the four of us and my team."

"Sally and Cody know a man was bothering me."

"I talked with both of them earlier in the day. They won't be telling anyone about this."

Kellie's father thanked him again. "I think it's time we left the two of you alone so you can get on with your plans. Come on, Nadine."

They both got up from the table. Kellie jumped up to hug them. "I'll call you all the time so you're not worried."

"We love you, honey."

"We do," her father said in a gruff voice and gave her a bear hug. "Do everything the Ranger says."

"I promise." She walked them to the front door. "I love you. Thank you for being the best parents on earth."

"I won't let anything happen to her," the Ranger assured them before they left the condo. The conviction in his voice prevented Kellie from breaking down.

Kellie shut the door and hurried past him to clear the table. He helped put everything in the waste bin while she wiped down the top. "If you want to get started on the blog piece, we can do it here."

"Sounds good, but let's sit down for a minute and lay the groundwork."

She nodded and followed his suggestion. He sat across from her. "First of all, I'd like you to call me Cy and I'll call you Kellie. Next, we need to make this real." He reached in his shirt pocket and set three rings on the table. After putting the larger gold band on the ring finger of his left hand, he said, "Go ahead and see if they fit."

With trembling fingers, she picked up the engagement ring with a beautiful one-carat diamond. She slid it on and it was a surprisingly good fit. So was the gold wedding band. The moment was surreal.

"How do they feel, Mrs. Vance?"

Her head flew back. Their gazes fused for a moment. *It feels too natural.* "Fine."

"Will they bother you when you ride?"

She blinked. "No. My right hand does most of the work."

"Good. Let's discuss the living arrangements. I plan

to sleep downstairs and had the team bring over a hide-a-bed couch. If you don't mind, I'll use the half bath on this floor, but I'll shower upstairs when you're not here. For the time being I'll use the guest room to store my clothes and equipment."

In the next breath he pulled a pair of latex gloves from his back pocket and put them on.

"Why don't you bring me the mail? I'll go through it in case this stalker has sent you a message to frighten you further."

At the thought, her body broke out in a cold sweat. Kellie went into the living room to get her purse and brought it to the table. After she opened it, he reached inside and took out the bills.

He went through the pile one piece at a time. "Let me know if you see something odd."

She shook her head. "It's the usual bills and ads."

He kept going. When he came to a *Cowboy Times* magazine, he held it up by the spine. Two cards fell out along with a three-by-five white envelope. He picked up the letter. There was no return name or address. Her name and address had been typed on the front. "This was postmarked from Austin on the same day he approached you in Eagle Mountain."

Kellie felt her stomach drop while she watched him open it. He spread out the eight-by-ten piece of folded paper. The word *liar* jumped out at them in big letters. She gasped. The stalker had cut them out of some magazine and had glued them on.

"This is going to the forensics lab. It's my opinion that over the years this man has had a string of broken relationships, maybe a failed marriage, and feels betrayed. He has no friends or anyone he's emotionally connected to. Every time he finds a new target, he convinces himself it's love. When nothing works out, he goes into a rage because every woman turns out to be a liar."

"I wonder how many other women he's done this to."

"Who knows, but it stops with you. I noticed you have a laptop upstairs. Why don't you bring it down and we'll get started on your announcement?"

"I'll be right back." When she brought it down a minute later, she noticed he'd put the letter in a plastic bag and had discarded the gloves. He'd also produced a laptop she'd seen lying on the hide-a-bed.

"I'd like to access more of your archives while you work on what you want to say."

"I'll send them to your computer." He gave her his address.

They worked side by side. She wrote something, then deleted it and started again. After several attempts she got into the blog-writing mode and allowed herself to go with the flow.

"How's it coming?" His deep voice broke the silence, but it continued to resonate inside her.

"It's almost there. I'll send you a copy in a minute to see what you think. After I've denied any involvement with a man, it's going to have to be convincing." She read over what she'd written so far.

Hi, all my faithful rodeo fans out there! I'm back from my last rodeo in Bandera, Texas, and won't be competing until two weeks from now in Rapid City, South Dakota, where I'll start out my Midwest circuit. My times have been up and down lately. But that's because something thrilling has happened to me in my personal life.

So many times you've asked me if I have a boyfriend or if I plan to get married one day. I've always said that my love life was private. But I can't keep quiet about this any longer. I did find the man of my dreams while I've been on the rodeo circuit. It was love at first sight for this gorgeous hunk of a cowboy. He's bigger than life to me and my hero in more ways than one.

We decided we couldn't stand to wait to get married until Finals in December. So we tied the knot in a private ceremony before my competition in Pendleton, Oregon. I'm so happy to be his wife, I go around in a daze. It's little wonder I've been unable to concentrate. Trixie thinks I'm a little crazy, bless her heart. It's a miracle she puts up with me and knows how to kill the cans in spite of me.

All of you know I always had a rule that I wouldn't allow a man to throw me off my game while I was riding the circuit. No distractions for me. No siree. But I hadn't met my husband when I said that. The second I looked into his eyes, my world changed in an instant. He's the prince I dreamed about when I was a little girl. He's the great man I'd hoped to meet while traveling the circuit around this great country of the USA.

We'll have a wedding reception after Finals. I'll post some pictures. You'll all swoon when you see him!

PS: Of course I want to win the championship, but

winning the love of my husband surpasses all else. I'm the luckiest cowgirl on the planet and grateful for all of you who constantly send me your support. Long live the rodeo!

Kellie saved the file and pushed the send button. In order to make her blog convincing, she'd had to put her heart into it. But while she waited for his opinion, heat crept into her cheeks. "I just sent you the announcement. While you check it for changes, I'll get a cola. Would you like one?"

"Sure. Thanks."

"Let me know what you think," she said and left the room.

Cy opened the file and started to read. His heart thudded when he came to the lines "The second I looked into his eyes, my world changed in an instant. He's bigger than life to me and my hero in more ways than one." The more he read, the harder his heart pounded.

"What do you think?" She put a cold can of cola in front of him. "I know it's probably too much, but I realize this has to convince my readers."

He opened his drink and swallowed half of it in one go. "I agree it's over-the-top, but it sounds like it came from the heart. When that creep reads this, it will push his buttons to the limit. The only correction is to delete Pendleton and put in Glasgow, Montana. That was your event before you left for Oregon. We don't want him to think his appearance in Pendleton had anything to do with the timing of your marriage."

She pulled the laptop in front of her and made the change. "I should have thought of that." Kellie smiled at him. "That's why you're one of the Sons of the Forty! Okay. It's done."

"Go ahead and post it. Now we wait. I wouldn't be surprised if your fans respond in droves and overload your website."

Cy finished off his drink and got up from the table to toss it in the wastebasket. He'd left her phone on the counter and brought it to her. "I checked your phone. The only call you received in the middle of the night came from a throwaway phone and couldn't be traced. I want you to continue to answer your phone.

"I've set it up with an app so you can record an incoming call. I'll walk you through this. It's easy." He pulled his own cell phone from his shirt pocket. "I'll call you. After you've answered, press Four and it will start recording. Ready?"

"Yes."

He pressed the digit that had programmed her number. She let it ring three times, then clicked on. "Hello?"

Cy nodded, letting her know to press the number four digit.

"Hi, Kellie. Did you just get back from Bandera?"

"I drove in this morning."

"How's Trixie?"

"She's at the ranch getting some TLC."

"I bet you wish you were with her."

"Tomorrow I'll drive out there and we'll go for a ride."

"Sounds fun. Talk to you later."

He held the phone away from his ear. "Now click End Call. The recording is downloaded to your iPhone and displayed on the screen. Tap the recording icon to listen. You can also trim the recording as needed by dragging the edge of the file on the screen."

She followed his directions and suddenly they heard their conversation while seeing it at the same time. A natural smile broke out on her lips. Good grief, she was beautiful. "Technology is amazing."

"In your case it's crucial. I want every word recorded when he phones you again."

"Do you think he'll try soon?"

Cy nodded. "If I don't miss my guess, he won't be able to hold back, not after what you've put on your blog."

"I'm afraid to talk to him." He noticed her shiver. "I don't think I'll be able to sleep tonight."

"Tell you what. Why don't you go upstairs and get ready for bed? Then come down here to sleep on the couch for tonight. I'll be nearby on the other couch. If he calls, I'll be right here. Try to get him to talk about why he thought you were lying to him. Anything he says could give us a clue about him."

"You wouldn't mind? I'm behaving like a baby."

"You're behaving like a woman who's being stalked. But I admire you for not giving in to your fear. That's what he wants. He's been watching you for a month if not longer and still doesn't believe you're married. But the blog entry will force him to reveal himself. The phone allows him a voice connection to you. Keep him on long enough for our voice experts to analyze it."

"What do you mean?"

"Vocal oscillations convey so much about the speaker. But more important, our experts will be able to tell if he's a Texan. A Texas accent stands apart from the rest of the South in that it has a twist that is a blending of the major features of the Deep South and Upper South."

"I didn't know that."

He nodded. "The drawl of the Lower South has more influence in East Texas, while the 'twang' of the Upper South has left a greater imprint on West Texas. In South Texas, particularly, the Spanish and Mexican characteristics are heavily combined with that of the others. Once we get a recording of his voice to the experts, they can tell us if he's from here or another state or region entirely. If we can pinpoint where he's from, it could be a great help."

"Then I'll try to keep him on the phone. Excuse me while I run upstairs to get ready."

"Take your time. We've got all night."

Cy planned to stay in the clothes he was wearing. Tomorrow he'd shower and change while she was out at her parents' ranch.

While she was upstairs, he sat down to see if there were any responses to her blog yet. A low whistle escaped when he counted seventy responses already. He scrolled through each one. When he came to the end, he was satisfied none of them was her stalker. It was touching to read how much her fans cared about her and appreciated her help through her online rodeo tips. But they were all excited about her marriage.

He opened up the archives. There were literally hun-

dreds of entries on her blog site. It amazed him. She
was definitely a star in her own right and an obvious
favorite. He knew she had dozens of awards, but she
didn't keep them here. Probably at the ranch. One thing
he knew about her already. There wasn't a narcissistic
bone in her lovely body.

While he read through a few more entries, she pad-
ded into the kitchen in bare feet wearing a blue robe.
Beneath it she wore pajamas with Texas Longhorns on
them. She'd brought down a blanket and pillow.

Cy had to be careful not to stare. "I take it you're a
football fan."

"These are from my parents last Christmas."

"My dad gave me a pair of the same pajamas two
years ago." They both laughed.

As she came closer, her smile faded. "Has that lunatic sent a response yet?"

"No. But you now have four hundred hits. Your eager
fans want pictures and don't want to wait until December."

Without saying anything, Kellie walked into the
living room and lay down on the couch, propping up
her pillow and covering herself with the blanket. Cy
checked his watch. It was ten to eleven. He picked up
her cell phone and put it on the coffee table in front of
her.

Once he'd made up the hide-a-bed, he went back to
the dining room for her laptop. After turning off the
overhead lights, he turned on a lamp in the living room
and sat down next to it so he could continue to read the
responses as they came in.

"When are *you* going to sleep?"

He liked it that she was concerned enough to ask and flicked her a glance. "Don't worry about me."

She sat up. Her disheveled hair gleamed in the soft light. "I don't know how to begin to thank you for what you're doing for me."

"It's my job."

"A horrible one," she said in a shaky voice. "Every day on the news you hear about some stalking victim found in a landfill—"

"Don't go there." Cy stopped her cold. "Nothing's going to happen to you."

"But who protects *you*?"

He smiled to himself. "I have a team that backs me up. My buddy Vic, one of the men you saw coming out of the radio station with me, is helping on your case."

She lay back down. "You're all remarkable."

"Save your thanks until after we've caught him."

Chapter Three

Kellie had no doubt he'd get the job done, but Cy Vance was too modest for words. That was part of the charm of the man who was growing on her with every passing second. His rugged profile stood out in the lamplight. He'd stretched out in the chair with his hard-muscled legs crossed at the ankles.

She'd been around cowboys all her life. Some of them were more attractive than others. Some had great builds. Others were loaded with talent in the arena. Still others had engaging personalities. But this Texas Ranger had all of those qualities and more. He'd been put together in such a way no one could compare to him.

Impatient with herself for concentrating on the attractive Ranger, she turned over so she faced the back of the sofa. She needed sleep. Desperately. Knowing he was right across the room from her gave her a sense of comfort she hadn't felt since her first encounter with the stalker. How unbelievable was it that the Ranger she'd bumped into in Bandera had come into her life at the most precarious moment of her existence?

When her cell phone suddenly rang, she jerked upright. Kellie flung herself around, staring at her phone in terror.

"It's all right." Cy's deep voice was reassuring. "What does the caller ID say?"

She took a shaky breath. "It's my best friend, Kathie."

"Go ahead and talk to her. Put it on speaker."

Kellie reached for it and clicked on. "Kathie?"

"Hi! I know it's late, but I had to call you. Good grief, Kellie. Is it really true that you're married?"

Her gaze locked with Cy's. "Yes. How did you hear?"

"Patty told me she read it on your blog tonight. How come you didn't tell me?"

Oh dear. Kellie heard the hurt in her voice. Now for the lie... But this lie was going to save her life and it took away her guilt. "It happened while I was on the circuit and there was no time." That part was true. "Look, Kathie. It's a long story and—"

"And your husband wants your attention. Is he right there?"

At that remark Cy's eyes smiled. Kellie felt a fever coming on. "Yes. We just got in from Bandera. I'll tell you all about it later."

"He must really be something for you to get married so fast you didn't even have your parents there."

"W-we couldn't bear to wait any longer."

"Whoa. I'll hang up now, but I expect a detailed report later. You know what I mean."

Embarrassment brought the heat in waves. "Thanks for calling. We'll talk soon. I promise." She clicked off and put the phone back on the coffee table.

Cy closed the laptop and put it on the floor. He leaned forward with his hands clasped between his knees. "Kathie is one of the names on the list you gave me. Who is she?"

"My best friend in our group. Sally, my other friend, is a part of it, too."

"What group is that?"

"There are about thirty of us who ride for pleasure, but serve as volunteers in case of any kind of local emergency."

His brows lifted. "Do you have a name?"

"We're the Blue Bonnet Posse."

"That's right. You mentioned one of your friends from the group who moved to Colorado Springs. Come to think of it, I have heard of the posse. Weren't you the ones who found that autistic child who'd wandered away from home last year?"

"That one, and a lost Boy Scout. The police department calls our leader when they need volunteers to do a search in the outskirts of Austin."

"No doubt you're kept busy. Those lucky parents must be indebted to you. I'm impressed."

"It's our job." She echoed his earlier words to her.

"Touché." He reached down and pulled off his cowboy boots. She watched him turn out the lamp and stretch out on the hide-a-bed. It couldn't be that comfortable, and he hadn't even changed. He lay on his back with his hands behind his head.

She forced herself to look away. But no sooner had she curled on her side hoping to fall asleep than the phone rang again. Still petrified, but less startled this time, she reached for the phone.

"Put the speaker on," Cy reminded her.

She nodded. It was her father and she clicked on. "Hi, Dad. I've got the phone on speaker."

"Forgive me for calling this late, but your mom and I want to make certain you're all right."

Her gaze drifted to Cy. "I'm fine. Really. The news is out. Kathie just called me."

"We got a call from your cousin Heidi. She read your blog and couldn't believe it."

"I know this is going to come as a shock to everyone who knows me."

"They care about you. It's a tribute to the wonderful woman you are."

"Spoken like a biased parent."

"We love you, Kellie." His voice sounded gruff with emotion. "Tell that Ranger we can't thank him enough."

She looked at Cy's silhouette in the semidarkness. "He knows how you feel. All I do is thank him."

"We're expecting you for lunch. Good night, honey."

"You get a good sleep, Dad. Cy is keeping me perfectly safe. Love you." She hung up the phone and hugged her pillow.

The next time she had cognizance of her surroundings, she heard the phone ringing. Immediately her adrenaline brought her to a sitting position. The second she realized there was no name on the caller ID, she felt bile rise in her throat. Cy had already hunkered down at the coffee table, urging her to pick up and press the recording app.

Her body shook as she reached for the phone. Doing as Cy asked, she clicked on. "Hello?"

"I knew you got home today. How did you like my letter?"

Her eyes closed tightly. "How did you get my phone and address?"

"That was easy as skinning a cat."

She shuddered. "What do you want? I told you I'm married."

"I saw what you wrote on your blog. You think I'd believe that crap? You're a liar!" He shouted the last word.

"You think I'd lie to all my fans and friends? If that's true, then why do you keep phoning a liar?"

"Because you deserve to be taught a lesson you'll never forget."

"Did your girlfriend lie to you?"

"They all lie. When I get through with you, you'll wish you'd never been born, Kellie girl."

"My husband's going to have a lot to say about that."

"Liar, liar, liar, liar, liar, liar!" The line went dead.

Kellie was trembling so hard she dropped the phone. Cy retrieved it and clicked on the recorded conversation. She'd forgotten to put on the speakerphone. His jaw hardened as he listened to the recording.

"That was rage we heard just now. He's afraid you might be telling the truth. You handled him perfectly and kept him on long enough to record his voice patterns. I'll be going into headquarters tomorrow. I'll drop off the letter at the forensics lab and take your phone to our voice expert to see what he can do with it."

He checked his watch. "It's only four in the morning.

Why don't you go up to your bed? If he phones again, I'll let it ring. You need more sleep."

"What about you?"

"I'm fine."

"Even if you aren't, you'd never tell me. Thank you." She grabbed her pillow and blanket before going upstairs.

Cy HAD SPOKEN prophetic words. The phone rang every half hour until eight on Tuesday morning. Then it stopped. He made breakfast with the groceries he and Vic had bought yesterday. While he devoured eggs and bacon, he phoned Vic on his phone. His friend answered before the second ring.

"What's up?"

"The stalker phoned her at four this morning. We were able to get a decent recording. When I'm back in the office, I'll have the lab analyze it. I'm headed there as soon as she leaves for her parents' ranch. I assume she'll be gone most of the day."

"The team will take turns monitoring her."

"Good. Where did you leave a car for me?"

"Walk down the alley behind the town houses to the corner. It's a Subaru parked in front of the third house on the right with a for-sale sign. The key is in the usual place."

"Do you think the lab has the results on the fingerprints we lifted yesterday?"

"Maybe. Stan said they'd hurry it."

"With all the bases covered, let's hope this nut case makes his move soon."

"Did you get any sleep last night?"

"Afraid not, but I will today after I get back from the lab. Kellie will probably be gone most of the day. I'll tell her to call me when she's coming back."

"You can level with me," he said in a quiet voice. "How's it going?"

He took a deep breath. "The easy answer is, nothing's going on that shouldn't."

Just then Kellie came walking into the kitchen dressed in Levi's jeans and a short-sleeved yellow blouse. She was a vision and he lost his train of thought.

"Cy? Are you still with me?"

"Yeah."

"I was just saying I can't wait to hear your difficult answer."

Neither could Cy, but this was pure business and that was the way it would stay. "Got to go. Thanks for your help. I'll catch up with you later at the office." He clicked off and stood to greet her. "Good morning. How do you feel?"

"Thanks to you I was able to go right to sleep."

"That's good news."

"But I bet you didn't get a wink." Her eyes had filled with concern.

"I'll make up for it later. Sit down and I'll serve you breakfast."

"I could smell the bacon. I should have gotten up to do it. Fixing food for me isn't your job."

"But you need more sleep than I do after what you've been through this last month." He put a plate of food in front of her and poured coffee for both of them before sitting down.

"Thank you, Cy." She ate a piece of bacon. "Yum. Crisp, just the way I like it. Were there any more phone calls from him after I went to bed?"

Cy eyed her directly. "He rang on the half hour eight times. I let it ring every time. Your marriage announcement has set him off, exactly the reaction I'd counted on."

"Did he leave messages on the voice mail?" There was a tremor in her voice.

"Yes, but you don't need to hear them. I'm taking your laptop and phone into the lab today, but I'll bring them back." The stalker probably had a stack of prepaid phone cards, but there might be a time when he had to use a pay phone that could be traced.

Her brows furrowed. "You think they're too awful for me to hear?"

"No. They were more of the same. He was ranting like before."

She sat back in the chair. "Then you really didn't get any sleep."

"I'll catch up today while you're at the ranch. Someone on the team will be monitoring you every time you leave your condo. A member of the crew will follow you. If you have any concerns, call me on your parents' phone. This is my cell number." He wrote it on the paper napkin.

"While I clean up the kitchen, I'd like you to get on your laptop. Post a new message on your blog. Say that you've read the messages and you're overwhelmed by all the good wishes. Then start to read any messages that have come since last night. I'm curious to see if he's posted anything. It's my hope he's so angry he might explode and give himself away."

As he cleared the table, she reached for her laptop and opened her blog file. "I don't believe it! Hundreds more messages have been added since last night."

"That's not surprising. Your online tips about barrel racing have won you a loyal audience. Everyone's intrigued about your new relationship."

She lifted her eyes to him. Along with her silver-gold hair, her eyes were a deeper blue this morning and dazzled him. "The fans want to hear about *you*, not me. If they knew you were one of the Sons of the Forty, they'd go crazy and you'd be forced to go into the witness protection program."

With those words his pulse sped up. "Hiding out with you is virtually the same thing."

He loaded the dishwasher. Cy had been a bachelor for so long in his own house, he was used to doing his own cooking and housekeeping. He felt right at home in her kitchen. "Why don't you start reading and see if there's a message that strikes a different chord with you?"

"It'll take me some time."

If they'd met under different circumstances, nothing would have pleased him more than to have whole days and nights with her with no life-threatening issue to deal with. But he had a case to solve and needed to get to headquarters pronto. As he was finishing up, he heard her cry out in alarm.

"What did you read?" He walked over to the table and stood behind her so he could see what had disturbed her. In looking over her shoulder, he could breathe in her fragrance from the shower.

"It's this one sent at eight twenty this morning."

"That's when the phone calls stopped. Read what it says."

"'I bet you're making it up that you have a husband. Why do you enjoy being a tease? No one would watch you in the rodeo if they knew you were such a liar.'" She let out a quiet gasp.

Without thinking, Cy put his hands on the back of her chair. He could tell she was trembling. "I'm going to stop him, Kellie. This morning he made his biggest mistake so far by posting this message on the blog. When I'm at the office, we'll trace it to its source. With every misstep, we're closer to catching him."

She nodded without turning around. He quickly removed his hands and walked over to the kitchen counter where he'd put her phone. He heard her chair legs scrape the tile and turned in her direction.

"I know you're anxious to get going, Cy. I'll run upstairs for my purse and leave for the ranch."

"I'll walk you out to the garage." While he waited for her, he put her phone in his pocket.

The door to the garage was located at the other end of the kitchen. He unlocked it and turned on the garage light where her white Toyota sedan stood parked. He and Vic had checked it for fingerprints yesterday.

When she came out, he opened the driver's side door for her. Once she was inside, he asked her for the remote. "I need it to get in and out with my own car. I'll let you in when you come back from the ranch."

Her eyes played over him as she handed it to him. "Where is it?"

"Parked around the block. Try to enjoy the day, Kellie. You'll be constantly watched. Call me from your parents' when you're ready to come home."

"I will. Have a good day yourself. Be careful," she whispered.

He took a quick breath. "You don't have to worry about me."

"But I do, and I *will*."

It had been a long time since a woman he cared about had been concerned about him. Her unexpected smile revealed the spirit inside her that had dominated her life and made her a champion. He admired her passion for life.

As she started the engine, he pressed the remote so the garage door would open. After she'd backed out, he retrieved his phone and alerted the surveillance team that she was leaving the condo.

Once he couldn't see her, he hurried inside for her laptop and the bagged letter. After he had everything he needed, he left through the garage, closed it with the remote and walked down the alley to the end. Eight-foot-high heavy-duty vinyl privacy fencing ran the length of the alley to separate the backyards of another set of town houses. It was a gorgeous September day, probably sixty-five degrees out.

He found the SUV and took off for headquarters. On the way to his office he stopped by the lab to leave Kellie's phone and laptop plus the letter. Stan came out to talk to him. "TJ said this is high priority. I'll get working on everything now and give you a ring later."

"Thanks, Stan. I need you to do something else for me. I want Rafe to analyze this stalker's voice and see what he can figure out."

"I'll ask him to work on it now and take a late lunch."

"I'd appreciate that. I don't see Janene. When she comes in, ask her to find out the IP for the person who sent Ms. Parrish the message on her blog. I've flagged it."

"Sure. I'll put it on her desk."

"Thanks. See you later."

Cy took off for his office upstairs. On the way down the hall, Vic saw him and called him into his office. "I've been waiting for you. I've got stuff to show you that will blow your mind. Look what the database brought up from the sketch you entered."

Intrigued by Vic's excitement, Cy grabbed a chair and sat next to him. "Thirty-two matches came up on the computer."

"Is there one from Oregon?"

"No."

"My first hunch was wrong, then," Cy muttered. "How about Utah, Montana, New Mexico or Texas?"

"None of those states."

Damn.

"Give me a second. I'm refining these for exact similarities."

Cy watched the screen. They both made sounds when two faces came up. After studying them he exclaimed,

"They're the same person with different rap sheets. How in the hell did that happen?"

Dean Linton Michaels, aliases Dan Linton, Dan Michaels, Michael Linton, Mick Linton, Delinn Michael, twenty-eight, latest known address in Flossmoor, Illinois, is wanted for the murder of two women. The first account is for the stalking and strangulation of a twenty-four-year-old woman, Lucinda Rosen, in Chicago, Illinois. The second account a year later is for the stalking and strangulation of a nineteen-year-old woman, Mary Ferrera, in Memphis, Tennessee. Charges include Aggravated Kidnapping, Unlawful Flight to Avoid Prosecution, Aggravated Sexual Assault. No. 10 on the FBI's most wanted list.

Vic darted him a glance before he scrolled down. "Take a look at this rap sheet."

Lines marred Cy's features as he found himself looking at what appeared to be the exact same man. This one had longer hair.

Andrew Dunham, aliases Denny Andrew, Andy Dunham, Drew Denning, Donny, twenty-eight, latest known address in New Orleans, Louisiana, is wanted for First-Degree Murder in the stalking and strangulation death of a twenty-three-year-old woman in Charleston, South Carolina, thirteen months ago. Charges include Aggravated Kidnapping, Unlawful Flight to Avoid Prosecution, Aggravated Sexual Assault.

Cy shook his head. "It's amazing how closely these two men resemble the sketch. There has to be a mistake since both pictures have to be the same person. Three murders in three years. Kellie needs to see these pictures. If he's the same man and the one she can identify... Let's get on the phone to the agents working those cases while we figure this out."

Over the next two hours they held phone conferences with the FBI agents from Illinois, Tennessee and South Carolina. In all three instances, the agents praised the Rangers for their detective work on Kellie's case and pledged their help.

After Cy's last call, he waited until Vic got off the phone. "I've sent both sets of fingerprints to Stan to verify if it's the same man. They say every person has a double somewhere in the world."

"I wonder if that's really true," Vic murmured.

"Who knows? I need to learn as much as I can before I show Kellie these photos. Even though the artist was able to find us a match, maybe he only bears a superficial resemblance to the man she saw." He printed out both photos. After folding them, he put them in his pocket. "Want to go down to the lab with me?"

Vic jumped up. "Try to keep me away."

When they entered the lab, Stan told them to come around to the table where he was working. They passed Rafe's office. He looked up. "I'm working on this voice analysis. Give me until tomorrow."

"Sure."

They moved toward Stan.

"You got some good prints lifted from the condo and

the car," he said. "Several belong to the victim, and several others belong to the mother. One partial print you lifted from one of the buttons of the keypad for the garage doesn't match anyone's."

Cy eyed Vic. "That's interesting. Maybe we'll find the person who left it. Right now we've got a new puzzle for you to solve. I just sent you the photos and fingerprints of two wanted fugitives who appear to be the same man from the IAFIS data base. But if they're the same man, why didn't the computer pick it up?"

"Let me see." Stan pulled up the information on the computer.

"Their cases have been built from two different areas of the country with different names. Their photos closely match Jim's sketch of the man stalking Kellie. How long will it take you to determine if both pictures are of the same man?"

"Give me a few minutes and I'll check right now." He put both sets of prints up on the screen and used his loupe and counter. He examined them for a while, and then his head came up. "Well, what do you know? Those men aren't the same person. This is a case of identical twins, but as you know there's no such thing as identical fingerprints."

Cy sucked in his breath. "That means both brothers are killers."

Vic looked equally stunned.

"It happens," Stan murmured. "Come close and I'll show you." He pointed to the subtle differences. "Fingerprints are not entirely a genetic characteristic. They are a part of a 'phenotype,' which means they are determined by the interaction of an individual's genes and the intrauterine environment. One fetus in the womb has different hormonal levels, nutrition, blood pressure, position and growth rate of the fingers at the end of the first trimester.

"Minor differences in fingerprints arise from random local events during fetal development. The genes determine the general characteristics of the patterns of fingerprints. However, inside the uterus, finger tissue comes in contact with the amniotic fluid, other parts of the fetus and the uterus.

"Some experts point out, for example, that touching amniotic fluid during the six to thirteen weeks of pregnancy significantly changes the patterns of a fetus's fingerprints.

"Overall, identical twins' fingerprints tend to be similar, but there always will be subtle differences making even their fingerprints unique. That's why there was no match."

Cy unconsciously furrowed his hair with his fingers. He felt the same as years ago when his chest had been stomped on by a bull. "If one of these twin brothers was the man who'd targeted Kellie, how am I going to tell her there are two of them? Hell, Vic. What if they work together and committed all three murders?"

"Maybe that's why the letter in her mailbox had been posted by the one brother here in Austin four days ago while the other brother trailed her all the way home from Oregon."

He eyed Vic. "The murders of the three women were committed a year apart at different places, making it possible that they'd worked in tandem." Cy's body broke out in a cold sweat.

Vic clapped his shoulder. "Take it easy. I know where your thoughts are headed, but it's too early in the process to go there. Like you said, maybe she'll say these photos don't look enough like the man who harassed her in Pendleton to make a definite identification. We know mug shots as well as sketches can be deceiving."

"Yeah. I know," he said in a wooden voice. He turned to Stan. "Do you think that partial print from her condo is substantial enough for you to detect if it matches one of these fingerprints?"

"That will take some time. I'll see what I can do with it."

"Thanks, Stan. Give me a ring no matter what you find. I'll be up in my office for a while longer."

"I'll go with you." Vic walked out of the lab with him.

In the space of a few minutes, Cy felt the full weight of this case to protect Kellie. During his career as a Ranger, he'd never been personally involved like this before. As the captain had warned him, this was a different kind of case for Cy. *You two will be walking a very thin line.*

Cy had no idea he could feel this gutted over the gravity of her situation. He couldn't think of her as just any woman who needed help. His feelings were more complicated than that, but he had an obligation to keep this situation straightforward. Yes, he was attracted to her and admired her great talent, but he couldn't allow that to interfere with his judgment and work ethic.

When they reached his office, Vic looked at him and said, "Go home, Cy. You haven't slept for twenty-four hours and won't be any good on this case without sleep."

"You're right. I'll leave now." He glanced at his watch. It was one thirty. "Kellie will be coming home this evening. I want to be there when she drives in. Thanks for everything, Vic."

"Hey—just doing my job."

"You do a lot more than that, and now I've got another favor to ask."

"Anything."

"Pick up her phone from Stan when he's done with it. I'll get it from you later."

"What's your next move?"

"If Kellie identifies this man as the one who approached her, I'm going to fly to Colorado Springs early in the morning and take her with me. She said she gave her cell-phone number to a friend of hers who works in the office of the Women's Pro Rodeo Association. The stalker had to get her cell phone number from someone.

"I checked out her friends and horse handler while we were at the town house yesterday. They haven't given her phone number to anyone, so I'm going to check out a hunch. We'll be back by evening at the latest. Keep a close eye on her place while we're gone."

"Will do."

"Thanks, Vic."

Cy left the building and hurried out to the car. He couldn't get to Kellie's town house fast enough. Once he'd parked in the garage, he rushed through the house to the upstairs bathroom for a shower and shave. After putting on a clean pair of jeans and a T-shirt in the guest bedroom, he felt better. All he needed now was some food.

He ate a couple of peanut-butter sandwiches and drank half a quart of milk. After putting his phone on the floor next to him, he collapsed on the hide-a-bed. He'd catch a couple of hours before she phoned. Cy had her garage-door opener and would have to let her in.

It felt as if he'd barely sacked out when his phone rang. He reached down for it and saw that his mother was on the line. In the midst of everything, he'd forgotten to tell his family that he'd gone undercover on a new case and wouldn't be available for a while.

That wasn't like him to let something so important slide. As he lay there, he realized he needed to get his act together in a hurry. Biting the bullet, he clicked on.

"Hi, Mom. How are you and Dad?"

"We're fine, darling. The point is, how are you?"

"I'm well, but I'm on a new case and have gone undercover."

"Oh, Cyril—we never see you anymore."

He knew his mother worried about the career he'd chosen, and she never failed to complain about it. But right now he didn't give her the chance.

"Sorry about that, but it's the nature of the job. I promise I'll leave messages to let you know I'm all right."

"I guess that means you can't come to the engagement party we're planning for Beth and Tom on Sunday night."

"I wish I could, but I'll have to wait to see them after this case is solved." He had to solve it. "Give everyone my love. I promise to call you soon."

Cy hung up and lay back again, letting out a heavy sigh. His sister was marrying Thomas Adamson in six weeks. He was an up-and-coming attorney in the law firm Cy's great-grandfather had established in Dripping Springs. Cy was meant to join the business, but law had never held any interest for him. He preferred law enforcement.

After high school, he'd gone the rounds with his father more times than he could count. To make matters worse, halfway through college he'd broken his engagement to a young woman whom his parents really wanted him to marry. He wasn't anyone's favorite son.

Cy fell back to sleep until the phone rang again. A look at the caller ID showed Bronco Parrish. It was Kellie's father. She was calling from the ranch. He clicked on and said hello.

"Hi" came her slightly breathless greeting.

"Are you coming home now?"

"Yes. I'll be there in ten minutes."

"I'll be waiting and open the garage door for you."

"Thank you. See you soon."

It was a long ten minutes. Unable to stand it any longer, he hurried through the house to the garage and opened it while he waited for her. His pulse picked up speed when he saw her drive in next to his Subaru SUV and turn off the engine. She got out of the car and walked toward him with a look that led him to believe she was relieved to see him.

He was relieved, too. Night had already fallen.

Chapter Four

"How's Trixie?" Cy asked after Kellie walked past him into the kitchen.

"Happy to be home. We had a good ride."

He shut and locked the door. "Have you eaten dinner?"

She swung around. "Yes." Her eyes searched his. "Any news yet?"

"Why don't we sit at the table? I have something to show you."

Kellie swallowed hard and sank down onto the nearest chair. He sat opposite her and pulled a paper out of his pocket. "The sketch Jim made was run through the IAFIS criminal database. This is what resulted."

He unfolded it and placed it in front of her. Her gasp filled the kitchen's interior. "That's the man! But his hair is longer here and he looks a little thinner than I remember."

Cy pulled out another paper and unfolded it. The second he put it in front of her, she jumped to her feet. "This one is exactly like I described to you and the artist. His hair is short here."

"There's no doubt in your mind?"

She stared at him. "I'm positive both photos are of the same man who approached me in Pendleton."

"That's all I need to know."

Kellie sat back down again. The photos had caused the blood in her veins to chill.

"We can thank God you came into the police station yesterday before anything happened to you."

Her hand went to her mouth. "It's the same man, so why are there different sets of names for him?"

He pocketed the papers. "It turns out they are identical twins."

She could hardly breathe. *"Twin murderers?"*

"I suspect they work together, but the FBI agents I spoke to didn't realize it until the forensics lab discovered that their prints weren't exactly the same. It would explain why you could receive a letter postmarked from Austin at the same time he approached you in Eagle Mountain."

Kellie buried her face in her hands, trying to comprehend it. The next thing she knew, he'd put a cup of coffee in front of her. "Drink this. You need it."

She took a deep breath and sat back in the chair. "Thank you." For a few minutes she sipped the hot liquid while she tried to absorb what she'd just learned.

"Tomorrow morning I'd like you to fly to Colorado Springs with me. Your friends have sworn they've never given out your cell-phone number to a soul. But if your friend at the Women's Pro Rodeo Association has put your number into the computer, that may explain where these men got it."

"You mean they hacked their computer?"

"I don't know. That's what I want to find out. You've been with that association for several years. These men know your rodeo schedule. Your name is on file with them. I'm curious to know if your friend kept your cell phone number to herself or put it in the computer, never thinking about it. Maybe she even saw him."

Kellie thought back. "When I gave it to her, she knew never to give it to anyone else."

"That was before she moved. Chances are she didn't put it in the system, but I need to find out."

She marveled at the way his mind worked. "What are you thinking?"

He leaned back in the chair drinking his coffee. "These stalkers are cunning. In order to talk to you, the one who approached you had to have done his homework. What you put on your website about belonging to the Women's Pro Rodeo Association might have given him an idea I want to explore."

Kellie had a feeling he hadn't told her everything. "What time do you want to leave?"

"At 5:30 a.m. We have a 7:00 a.m. flight. If we get our business done fast, you'll be back here in time to put your horse through some maneuvers before evening. This will be our first venture in public as a married couple, so we'll behave as man and wife when we reach Colorado."

Man and wife. A tremor ran through her body. He'd anticipated every question and had answered them before she could even think.

"Then I'm going to get ready for bed now."

"Before you go upstairs, I want you to walk out to the mailbox and bring in any mail you find. Don't worry. One of the team will be watching you. I'll be waiting by the front door."

She got this sick feeling in her stomach over the idea that the stalker might have been near her condo today. Reaching in her purse for her keys, she left the town house and took the short walk to retrieve her smattering of mail from the box.

After she returned, she walked over to the table and put it down. There were three ads, a catalog of home decor furnishings and a five-by-seven white envelope with nothing written on the front. When she saw that it didn't have a stamp, she froze.

"When does your mail normally come?"

"Between two and three."

"The stalker may have come after to slip this into your box."

"You think he had a key?"

"These criminals are professionals and have tools, but we're going to find out."

Cy put on gloves and picked it up. After opening the flap, he pulled out a black-and-white glossy photograph of Kellie taken in a beauty salon. She was sitting in a chair with a drape around her neck. Her head had been cut out and it fell on the table. The word *liar* had been printed on the back of it.

"I don't believe it!"

He gave her a probing glance. "Where was this taken?"

"At a beauty salon here in Austin where I go to get my hair styled."

"How long ago?"

"Right before I left for Montana, about five and a half weeks ago."

"You're sure about the timing?"

"Yes. Normally I wear cowboy boots all the time and I always get my hair done later in the day. But that particular morning I had an early appointment and I put on those sandals before I left for the salon because I was in a hurry."

"What time was your appointment?"

"Eight thirty in the morning."

"Do you remember the date?"

"It was a Wednesday. I had to leave right after to make it to Glasgow in time for the rodeo on Saturday, August 2."

"That meant you were in the salon on July 30. How big is the place?"

"It does a lot of business. The Blue Gardenia is on Third Street downtown."

"I've heard of it. Do men get their hair cut and styled there, too?"

"Yes." She shuddered. "That means he was in there watching me. He probably has dozens of pictures of me. It's sickening and depraved."

"Stay strong, Kellie. We're going to catch him."

A moan escaped her. "What about his twin?"

When she looked at him, the dark blue of his eyes seemed to have turned black. "Him, too. Go on up to bed and set your alarm. We'll leave for the airport at five thirty. Before we walk out the door, I'll turn on the camera over the kitchen door on the garage side."

"You think he'll come while we're gone?"

"I'm not sure."

He obviously had more work to do she wasn't privy to, so she got up from the table. "I don't know how to thank you for what you're doing. Your life is in danger, too."

"But this is my job. One I like, though no one in my family does."

"What did they want you to be?"

"An attorney like my father and his father and his father before him."

So Cy was the lone wolf… His own person. She liked that about him very much.

"When this whole ghastly ordeal is over, I'll tell your family personally that you have the undying gratitude from me and my family for coming to my rescue."

His intense gaze continued to hold hers. "That's nice to hear. Now try to get some sleep and leave the worrying to me."

THE SECOND SHE disappeared upstairs, Cy phoned the crew in the surveillance van. "Lyle? The stalker put an envelope in Kellie's mailbox today. There are eight tenants using that box. Did anyone approach it you can't identify?"

"Yes. A woman with dark brown hair. I checked with the landlord of the property. He's never seen her."

A *woman*. "Strange. What time did the camera record it?"

"Four twenty."

That was after the mail had been delivered. "Send me a picture."

"There are three of them. Doing it right now."

As they came through his phone, he studied them. The person was dressed in a woman's business suit with low heels. She would be the same height Kellie had described for the stalker. Any view of the face gave only a partial glimpse. The lab could magnify the images for a better look.

"Lyle? Send these to forensics for enlargements."

"Will do."

"Tomorrow I'll be in Colorado Springs part of the day with Ms. Parrish. That'll give the stalker time to case the town house. He may try to get in to find out if a man lives here with her. Maybe the stalker's twin will show up, too. It's possible they dress in drag part of the time. Keep me posted."

"Sure thing."

Cy ended the call and phoned Vic. "It's possible one of the twins has been dressing up as a woman. I'm sending you the photos taken by Ms. Parrish's mailbox. Go over to the Blue Gardenia beauty salon on Third Street when it opens tomorrow. Show these pictures to everyone who works there. I'm curious if one of the employees can identify our stalker, who likely used his phone camera to take a picture of Kellie getting a haircut." Cy gave him the time and date. "If you get any information from one of the workers at the salon, let me know.

"Then I want you to call around to the places where you can buy a wig. Take those mug shots with you.

The photograph taken of Kellie was snapped almost six weeks ago. See if our stalker purchased one or two wigs in different colors during the month of July and get a copy of the receipt. It's a long shot, but do what you can."

"I'll try everything including places that sell theatrical makeup. He could have posed as an actor needing makeup and a wig."

"Exactly. Thanks, Vic."

"When will you get back from Colorado Springs tomorrow?"

"I'm not sure. Kellie needs to exercise her horses, so I'll drive her to her parents' after we get off the plane. But I'll phone you."

ON WEDNESDAY MORNING Kellie got out of the rental car and walked alongside Cy as they entered the building that housed the WPRA in Colorado Springs. She welcomed the warm seventy-nine-degree temperature. Conscious she was playing a part as Cy's new wife, she'd worn a flirty skirt and dressy blouse with high heels to play up her feminine side. It felt good to put on something besides jeans and cowboy boots.

"May I help you?"

"I'm here to see a friend who works here," Kellie told the attractive, twentyish-looking receptionist who hadn't taken her eyes off Cy from the moment they'd walked in the foyer. In a business suit and tie, he'd drawn the attention from a lot of women during their flight.

"Her name is Olivia Brown." Kellie prodded the younger woman in case she hadn't heard her the first time.

"Oh, sure. She's the one who moved here from Texas and works in the membership auditor's office. I'll ring her. You know? You kind of sound like her."

Kellie happened to glance at Cy, who was smiling at her rather than the receptionist. Even his eyes smiled, sending a charge of electricity through her body.

"Olivia wants to know your name."

Gathering her wits, she said, "Tell her it's a friend from the Blue Bonnet Posse."

The receptionist passed it on and suddenly red-haired Olivia came running down the east hallway. "Kellie!" she called out and ran up to give her a hug. "I can't believe it!" She turned to the girl at the desk. "Janie? This is the very famous Kellie Parrish! She's going to win the barrel-racing championship at Finals in Las Vegas this December."

"Wow." Janie's eyes had rounded in surprise.

"One could hope," Kellie murmured in an aside.

"Who's the stud?" Olivia whispered.

Kellie's heart was palpitating out of her chest. "I'd like you to meet my new husband, Cyril Vance."

"You got *married*?" Her voice came out more like a squeak.

"We did," Cy said and shook her hand.

"I announced it on my blog."

"Let me see." Olivia grabbed Kellie's left hand, then whistled. "Gorgeous." She looked up. "I haven't had a chance to read it yet. Oh, how wonderful. Congratulations!" She hugged her again. "Come on down to my office. I'm dying to know what brings you two here. If you're on your honeymoon, I can't figure out how come I'm lucky enough to deserve a visit."

Cy cupped Kellie's elbow and squeezed it as they followed Olivia down the hall.

"Come on in and sit down. Do you two want coffee or soda?"

"Nothing, Olivia. We ate before coming here, but thank you. There's a specific reason why we're here. I'll let Cy explain. My husband is a Texas Ranger working on a case that involves me."

After a five-minute explanation, there were no more smiles coming from Olivia. He showed her a paper that included both mug shots. "These men are identical twins. Do you recognize either of them?"

"No. I've never seen them."

"Do me a favor and show this to everyone who works here. If they've seen them, phone me immediately." He wrote his work number on the paper. "If one of these men had come around here, it could have been as far back as a year ago."

"I'll do it today." She looked at Kellie. "You poor thing. I'm ill over what you've just told me. Let me get into the records on the computer. I always update the information on a file when rodeo results come in. I've been here eighteen months. If I added your cell phone, I don't remember doing it."

"Does everyone on the staff have equal access to the files?"

"No. Only certain of us have the password to get into them." She opened the file.

Kellie wasn't aware she'd been holding her breath

until Olivia looked at them with a pained expression on her face. "Oh no—I *did* put your number in next to your parents' number. I remember now. I put it there for me, never dreaming anyone would ever see this file but me."

"Please don't worry about it, Olivia."

"It could be a blessing in disguise." A somber look had stolen over Cy's features. "Do you know the company that cleans this building?"

"Yes. It's called Grayson Janitorial Services."

"When do they clean?"

"At night after nine."

Kellie turned to him. "You think the stalker pretended to be a janitorial worker and got into the computer?"

"Maybe. If he's cyber savvy, it's a distinct possibility he broke in." His gaze swerved to Olivia. "We're going to go there now and talk to the owner."

"Let me give you the address." Olivia looked it up on the computer and wrote it down on some scratch paper to give to him.

"Thank you. Before we leave, I need one more piece of information. What company services your computers?"

"It's Standard Computer Services."

"We'll find it. Thank you, Olivia. Your help has been invaluable."

"I wish I could have helped you more. I pray you catch that stalker. It's too horrible."

"Cy is keeping me sane," Kellie confessed. "Give my best to your husband. We'll talk soon." They hugged once more before Cy escorted her out of the room and down the hall to the entrance.

"Good luck!" Janie called out. "I hope you win."

"Thank you."

They walked outside and Cy helped her into their rented Buick sedan. Using the Google mapping system, they drove across town to Grayson Janitorial.

Kellie glanced at Cy. "I know Olivia was upset that she'd put my cell number in the database."

"As I said, if this helps me trace the stalker's steps, it could uncover valuable information. It's like putting a puzzle together. Every piece I find forms the picture. If I'm on the wrong trail, we'll head over to Standard Computer Services. Maybe they sent out a technician to the WPRA who resembles our stalker."

Once Cy had parked the car, he took her arm and they entered the business. The store was filled with janitorial supplies. He flashed his credentials in front of the man at the counter.

"I need to speak to the owner."

"Just a minute." The man made a phone call. "A Texas Ranger is out here needing to talk to you."

When he hung up, he told them to walk around the counter and through the closed door to the back office. The middle-aged owner got up from his seat behind the desk and shook their hands. Cy wasted no time pulling out another paper and showing it to the owner.

"Have you ever hired either of these men to work for you? It could have been as far back as six months to a year ago. I'm following up a lead on a case. I understand your company cleans the offices of the WPR Association."

"That's right." The other man studied the mug shots before shaking his head. "I'm the only person who hires and assigns the work for my employees. I've never seen these men."

"What if one of your employees took a friend along while he or she worked?"

"That's against the rules, but I'll talk to my crews. Can I keep this paper?"

"I want you to. I'll write my work number on it in case you have information for me. Thank you."

Cy put an arm around Kellie's back as they left the office. It felt so natural, she didn't think about it until they'd reached the car. While he looked up the address for the computer company on his phone, she glanced at the striking man behind the wheel. She wondered if he could be aware of her in the same way she was of him. When she'd introduced him as her husband to Olivia, she'd felt a sense of pride. *Because you're attracted to him, Kellie, and you're getting too comfortable around him.*

He started the car and drove to another part of the city, where he parked in the lot next to the building reserved for Standard Computer Services.

"Cy? If you want, I'll wait here while you go inside."

His head turned to her, impaling her with those dark blue eyes. "Until I arrest the stalker, I'm not letting you out of my sight."

The way he said it caused a shiver to run through her body. "I just thought—"

"It's my job to keep you safe," he broke in. "I brought you to Colorado to introduce me to Olivia. There's no way I'd leave you sitting alone in this car."

Of course he wouldn't! A killer was after her.

She undid the seat belt and got out of the car before he could come around to help her. For a minute she'd been so concentrated on him and so worried he sensed her attraction to him, she'd said something that had probably made him question her mental capacities. *Get a grip, Kellie.*

He accompanied her inside the building. When he made inquiries, one of the guys working the counter showed them to the manager's office. It was like déjà vu. After introductions, Cy asked the manager to search through their work orders for the WPR Association going back a year.

"This will take me a minute."

"That's all right. I want you to be thorough." While they waited, Cy pulled another paper out of his pocket.

"It looks like we've sent our technicians out there four different times."

"Tell me the dates."

Kellie heard him mention January, April, June and July.

"Do you send one technician at a time?"

"Almost always."

Cy handed him the paper. "Have either of these men worked for your company within the last year? Take your time."

The manager took it from him. Within seconds he looked up at Cy. "This one with the longer hair. His name was Denny Denham." Kellie let out a soft gasp. "He applied for work in April, but only stayed until the end of June."

"Denny Denham has many aliases. He's on the FBI's most wanted list and killed a woman." The manager dropped his jaw in shock.

Kellie's heart thudded painfully. Cy's hunch had paid off. At this point she was in awe of his genius.

"Why did he quit?"

"He said his mother was in a hospital in Michigan and needed him."

"Was he a good tech?"

"Very good. I didn't like losing him."

"Was he the tech sent to the WPRA offices on any of the dates you gave me while he was still working for you?"

"I'll have to go through the signed receipts. It'll take me a few minutes."

"Go ahead."

Cy flashed Kellie a smile meant to encourage her that they were on the right track. He could have no idea of the emotions that smile stirred up inside her.

The manager looked at Cy. "Denny signed the work order for June 20. It was right after that he had to quit work."

The set of Cy's hard jaw spoke volumes. "I want to see his application."

"I'll print it out."

Cy took the paper and stood to shake the manager's hand. "You've been very helpful on this case. Thank you."

The manager still looked dazed as they left the office. Once in the car, Cy started the engine. "I've got everything I came for. We'll head back to Austin in time for you to get in some training with your horses. En route to the airport would you like to stop for a hamburger at a drive-through?"

"That sounds good."

"I got lucky today. That always gives me an appetite."

"It's not luck, Cy. You're brilliant. Didn't you want to study his work application before we left?"

"I'll pore over it with Vic after we get back. It'll be filled with lies, but maybe there'll be something in it that will be valuable to the agents working on the other murder cases."

She stared out the window. "That poor manager looked shattered. Surely he did a background check."

"I have no doubt of it. The trouble with criminals is that they're human beings just like everyone, and for most of the time they drift in and out of the shadows without anyone realizing it until it's too late."

Kellie's gratitude for Cy and all he was doing caused her throat to swell. "I'll never be able to thank you enough, and don't tell me it's nothing."

A low chuckle came out of him. "I wasn't going to. Since taking your case, I've become a husband. I never dreamed it was such a responsibility."

"You're probably sorry you got involved to this extent."

"I wouldn't have done it if it wasn't exactly what I felt needed to be done."

"But I feel guilty because it makes it difficult for you to have a personal life."

"Don't worry about that. I've had a personal life and barely escaped getting married."

Her head swung toward him. "Seriously?"

He nodded. "Her name was Eileen Richards. We were engaged, but it didn't feel right to me and I broke it off."

"How long ago?"

"I was twenty-one and halfway through undergraduate school."

Kellie imagined he was in his early thirties now. "That's young."

"Yup. But my parents and her parents were all for it. As I told you before, they had my life planned out to be an attorney. To everyone's displeasure, once I'd said goodbye to her, I left school and signed up with the Austin police department. I discovered I didn't want to defend criminals, I wanted to catch them."

"Thank heaven," she whispered. "How long have you been a Ranger?"

"Almost three years and I've never regretted my decision. To answer your next question, Eileen is married to a successful businessman. According to my mother, she's expecting her second child, and I couldn't be happier about it."

Neither could Kellie.

Once they'd eaten a quick lunch, they dropped off the rental car and caught their flight back to Austin. They walked to the short-term parking for Cy's car and headed for her parents' ranch.

"We made good time, Cy. It's only four o'clock."

"That's why I wanted to get away early this morning."

She gave him directions and soon he'd pulled up in front of their ranch house. "Would you like to come in? I know my parents would like to talk to you."

"Another time and I will, but I've still got a lot of business to do. Don't forget that one of the crew always keeps you in his sights."

"I know. I'll ask my parents to drive me to the town house tonight."

"Give me a call. I'll be waiting for you."

He had no idea what that meant to her, but he was probably tired of hearing it and she could tell he was anxious to leave. She climbed out of the car and hurried to the front door. Opening it, she called out, "Mom?"

"In the kitchen, darling."

Kellie wheeled around and waved to Cy. He waved back and drove off. She stared after him, wishing she didn't feel strange when his car disappeared. As if she'd lost something.

Her mom gave her a hug. "You're back earlier than I would have expected."

She took a deep breath. "Cy accomplished what he needed. Where's dad?"

"He's out in the pasture, but he'll be back by six."

"Then I'll have enough time to do some training drills with Trixie before dinner."

Her mother followed her up the stairs to her old bedroom. "What happened today?"

Kellie walked over to the dresser where she kept

her older clothes and pulled out a top and some jeans. "He found out how the stalker got my cell-phone number." While she changed outfits, she told her mom everything. "He's so amazing, I couldn't believe it. Talk about methodical. His mind works differently than the average person's.

"I found out his parents wanted him to go into law, but he broke his engagement to this girl and left college to join the Austin police department. He knew what he wanted and went after it. Now he's a Texas Ranger." She stared at her mom. "He can be formidable, but it's cloaked in sophistication. He told me he was going to catch this stalker."

Her mother eyed her pensively. "You believe in him."

"Utterly. He's incredible. I've never met anyone like him."

"No. Neither have I. Your cousin wants to hear all about him."

Kellie nodded. "I'll call her tonight when I get back to the town house. Has anyone else phoned?"

"Yes. Besides many of your friends, news of your marriage has prompted the *Statesman* and the *Chronicle* to get in touch with you for a story and a photo op. Even Tammy White from Hill Country Cowboy Radio is asking for another interview. She said you were a dark horse for pretending that you didn't know Cyril Vance when you were already married to the gorgeous Texas Ranger."

Heat crept into her face. "What did you tell everyone?"

"That you'd get in touch with them when you had time."

"Thanks, Mom. You're an angel." She pulled on a pair of cowboy boots she kept in her closet. "I've got to get out there so Trixie won't think I've abandoned her. See you in a little while."

She flew out of the room and down the stairs. Once she left the house, she ran all the way to the barn. But her thoughts weren't on Trixie. They were concentrated on the man who'd be at the town house later tonight to let her in. She found she was breathless just thinking about it.

Chapter Five

Pleased to discover that Vic was already at the town house, Cy drove into the garage, anxious for them to share information. His friend was dressed in the roofer uniform he'd worn the other day. He'd parked the roofing truck near the end of the alley.

"You got back earlier than I'd thought," Vic said as Cy entered the kitchen.

"That's because I found the information I wanted." He removed his jacket and tie and laid them over one of the chair backs, then he grabbed a soda from the fridge. "Do you want a cola?"

"Sure." They both took a long drink. "I brought Kellie's phone back, but she'll have to wait for her laptop," Vic informed him.

He saw it lying on the table. "Good. She'll be glad to have it." Cy reached for it and checked the messages. The stalker had sent three more. He put on the speakerphone so Vic could hear them, too. It was more of the same enraged vitriol.

Cy swallowed more of his drink. "I have news. Kellie's friend put her cell-phone number in the WPR Association's database. After some searching I discovered that a Denny Denham worked for Standard Computer Services as a tech in Colorado Springs starting in April of this year. He was called out on a problem at WPRA and signed the work order June 20. After that, he quit his job on the excuse he needed to be with his sick mother in Michigan."

Vic's whistle sang throughout the kitchen. "I talked to Rafe. Get this. He said the voice on Kellie's phone meets the criteria for a person from Virginia Beach or Charleston, South Carolina."

"A long way from Texas," Cy mused aloud. "Charleston's the place where one of the victims was killed."

"Yup. The minute I heard that, I started a search of all identical twin boys born in both the Virginia Beach area and the Charleston area over the time period I've estimated. I'm waiting for them to get back to me."

"You do great work. At this point I'm wondering where these killers saw Kellie and decided to target her. Until now they've operated in the other half of the US."

"You'll figure it out. In the meantime Stan told me that he couldn't get a good read on the half fingerprint from the garage-door pad."

Cy's eyes closed for a minute. "That was a long shot. Did the woman show up at the mailbox today?"

"No. Nothing went on around the town house. It's a waiting game now."

"I'm pretty sure he'll break in one of these nights, possibly even tonight after he sees Kellie's parents drop her off. I'll be waiting for him."

"Or them," Vic added. "The crew will cover the front of the condo. I'll be out in back."

"Any news on the IP address of the email sent to Kellie?"

Vic shook his head. "Janene's still working on the source. Tor hidden services mask their locations behind layers of routing. But she got into a site called 'hangman' and discovered the owner had left the administrative account open with no password. She logged in and is still digging around. As soon as I hear from her, I'll let you know."

"Good." Cy reached into his pocket and pulled out the paper from the computer services company. "This is the application the stalker filled out to get hired for work at the computer company."

They sat down at the table to study it. Cy let out a harsh laugh. "Look at that reference. As I told Kellie, it's full of lies. Two years at another computer company in Omaha, Nebraska, before he moved to Colorado Springs?"

"I'll call the number and see who answers." Vic pulled out his cell phone and tried it, then put the phone to Cy's ear. "You may have reached this recording in error. You can try again or call your operator." Vic hung up.

Cy rubbed his eyes with the palms of his hands. "No doubt he used his brother, who set up a phony address and phone to send the referral. These killers get around, Vic. They've got money to operate. Most likely smash-and-grab stuff, unless they're living off a family death benefit of some kind. I'll email this to the agents on the East Coast."

"Depending on what goes on here tonight, I'll track things down tomorrow." Vic checked his watch. "Tell you what. I'm going to leave to get me a bite to eat. But I'll let you know when I'm back for the rest of the night."

"I can't do this without you." Cy walked him to the back door. After Vic left, he phoned TJ to check in and catch him up on the latest.

"If two of them break in, you may need more backup."

"Vic and the crew have us covered."

"I'll put two more Rangers on alert anyway," his boss said before Cy heard the click.

A second later his phone rang. The caller ID said Nadine, Kellie's mother. He picked up. "Kellie?"

"Hi." The small tremor in her voice brought out his protective instincts.

"Is all well with you and your horses?"

"They're in fine form." She'd ignored his question about herself. The tension had to be getting to her. "I just wanted you to know my parents are driving me home now. We should be there in five minutes."

"Good. Before you come in the house, check your mailbox."

"I will. See you soon." She hung up.

He got up from the table and walked into the living room while he prepared himself for what might happen tonight. If the stalker suspected Kellie had been telling the truth about a husband, he might lie low so she would think the menace had gone away. But neither he nor his twin would ever go away. One thing about a sociopath. Once he'd fixated on his victim, he'd dog her to the bitter end no matter how long it took. With two sociopaths working together, they were a lethal combination.

He ground his teeth, hoping both of them showed up. Once they were taken down, Kellie could get on with her life. So could he...

While he was trying to imagine what that would be like now that he'd met her, he heard her key in the lock. In order not to frighten her, he moved to the kitchen so she'd see him when she walked in. After she locked the door behind her, she turned around.

He noticed she was wearing her riding clothes and boots. Kellie's eyes flew to his. She held up a couple of catalogs. "This was all I found in the box." She put them on the kitchen table.

Cy thumbed through them, but there was no envelope hiding inside the pages. He looked up. "Have you eaten dinner?"

"Ages ago."

"Why don't you sit down and tell me what's wrong? Did something happen you need to talk to me about?"

Her chin lifted. "What's wrong is that you're putting your life on the line for me," she said in a voice shaking with emotion.

He cocked his head. "Would you rather someone else were doing this job? It can be arranged."

"No!" she cried out. "No," she said in a softer tone and looked away. "That isn't what I meant at all."

"Then what *did* you mean?" came his deep, almost-seductive voice.

She folded her arms to her waist. "Situations like this shouldn't happen to anyone, but I know they do. Horrible things happen all the time, all over the world, and a handful of men and women like you are courageous enough to make the bad people go away. There isn't a way to repay you for what you have to face twenty-four hours a day in order to protect someone like me."

Cy put his hands on one of the chair backs. "I get my payment every time I lock up a criminal and throw away the key. There's no satisfaction like it."

"Then you're an amazing breed of man."

"That's exactly what I was thinking about you when I saw you perform in Bandera. Only a few exceptional women have the patience and the skills to work year in and year out to thrill the thousands of people who can only dream about what you do on your horse. The heart of a champion is inside you. All I could do watching you at the rodeo was sit back and marvel."

She eyed him with a frank stare. "What you do and what I do aren't comparable, but I appreciate the compliment."

"It was heartfelt."

"You enjoy the rodeo?"

"All my life."

Her eyes lit up. "Really?"

"I love it. Growing up we had horses and always went to the rodeo. I still keep my horse on my parents' small ranch and ride when I have time. Like most of my friends when I was young, I thought it would be fun to try bull riding and calf roping. But our pitiful attempts that ended in pain and suffering let me know it takes a lot more than just wanting to do it. You know…like possessing the skill, like being born to it, like having the guts to go at it again and again."

Her chuckle delighted him. "That's my father."

"Some of us have it. Some of us don't."

"Instead, you face a terrifying human enemy with no thought for your own life."

Cy laughed. "Don't be deceived. I give a lot of thought to my own life, believe me."

Her smile slowly faded. "I've given a lot of thought to your life, Ranger Vance. Please take care of yourself." The throb in her voice resonated inside him. "It's almost ten o'clock. Unless you need me for anything, I'm going to go upstairs."

He reached for her phone and handed it to her. "You can have this back. Forensics got what they needed from it, but they still have your laptop. I've removed all the messages."

She gripped it. "Did they find a voice match?"

"Yes."

"A Texan accent?"

"No. The stalker sounds like certain people who live in either Virginia Beach or Charleston, South Carolina."

Kellie's surprise over the news caused her to groan. "Charleston was the place where he killed one of his victims."

"Listen to me, Kellie. If I have anything to do with it, there won't be any more."

She nodded. "As I told my mother earlier today, I believe in you. Now I'm going to call some of my friends who left messages with my mom."

"After you do that, turn the ringer off. If the stalker intends on calling you tonight, I don't want you bothered by him. You need sleep."

A pained expression broke out on her face. "What are you going to do?"

"Coordinate with my backup crew."

She slid him an anxious glance. "You think something might happen tonight?"

He watched a nerve throbbing at the base of her throat. Cy was determined to make her fear go away. "If not tonight, perhaps tomorrow night or the next. Either way we'll be ready."

"Then I'll say good-night."

"If you need me, phone me. But by no means come downstairs until I let you know it's all right."

"Okay." She held his gaze for a moment longer before she went upstairs. Soon after, Cy's phone rang. It was Vic.

"I'm walking down the alley to the garage."

"I'll open it."

"Did you know the boss has supplied extra backup?"

"He told me."

"Chris and Jose will be in a taxi in the alley. Lyle and the rest of the crew are in place."

"Good. We're set. This is the window of time the stalker has been waiting for. I'm counting on his making a move any night this week. Next week he knows she'll be leaving for Colorado. If he thinks she could be married, he's got to find out and get rid of her husband before he takes her off someplace and strangles her. He'll need his brother."

"Yup."

"See you in a minute."

Cy hung up and went out to the garage. He lifted the door partway. In less than a minute, Vic came crouching in before Cy lowered it. They both walked through the garage and kitchen to the living room.

"Has Kellie gone to bed?"

"As far as I know."

"How's she handling it?"

"The woman is tough. I'm beginning to understand why she's such a fierce competitor in the arena. That's the only reason this setup is working."

"I think it's more a case of the right two people being thrown together."

Cy knew where his friend was going with that remark, but now wasn't the time. "The thing I keep wondering about is why this pervert targeted Kellie specifically. Her beauty provides one obvious answer. But there's more to it than that. Nothing we've learned so far, not even after collaborating with the FBI agents back east, has shed any light. I'm trying to find the missing link."

"Maybe it will have to come after we catch them."

"You're right." He glanced at Vic. "What do you say we do this in shifts? I'll take the first watch." He fixed the hide-a-bed so Vic could stretch out when he was ready. "Since we know there's no side or back door to this place, my hunch is he'll come in through the garage with a device to let himself in the door into the kitchen."

Vic nodded. "That makes the most sense. The fence isn't that high. He'll be able to scale it easily. I did a patrol of the town houses on the other side of the alley. The tenants don't have garages and park their cars in covered parking across their street. If someone wanted to hide out, they'd have to jump the fence from this alley into one of the backyards and wait so they wouldn't be seen."

After talking strategy for a while, Vic lay down. Cy turned out all the lights in the condo before going into the kitchen. He took out his .357-caliber SIG Sauer and put it on the table. After pouring himself a hot mug of coffee, he sat down in front of his laptop in the dark. Time to catch up on the paperwork for Kellie's case while he could still remember times and details of their trip to Colorado.

Once he'd finished, he went back to Kellie's website and scrolled through her scheduled events, starting with the first rodeo of this year. To his shock he discovered she'd entered the Salem, Virginia, Annual Stampede on January 9. His adrenaline surged.

She'd gone back east!

Cy should have thought about that before now, but he'd been so concentrated on the months since the stalker had appeared, only now had he started to explore all the possibilities.

After consulting a Virginia map, he saw that Salem was on the opposite side of the state from Virginia Beach.

He scrolled down quickly. More shocks. She'd ridden in the Walterboro, South Carolina, Rodeo two weeks after leaving Virginia. Cy looked up the South Carolina map. Walterboro was only forty minutes away from *Charleston*.

Were the stalkers born in Charleston? Did they call it home when they weren't victimizing women? Vic was still waiting to hear back on the identical twins most likely born there or the Virginia Beach area. His friend was asleep, so Cy would have to wait to discuss the idea with him later.

Needing to do something with all the energy flooding his system, he kept scrolling for more information. On the first weekend of February she rode in the Chatsworth, Georgia, Rodeo. Mid-February she entered the rodeo in Memphis, Tennessee, where another murder had taken place.

In March she'd participated in rodeos throughout the Midwest before returning to Austin via a rodeo in Hampton, Arkansas, and another one in Fort Worth, Texas. But his mind kept going back to the Walterboro Rodeo.

If for some reason the stalkers had gone to the rodeo that night, they would have seen Kellie, who had the best time during the performance that night. That might have been the place they first decided she'd be their next target.

Unless—and it was a big *unless*—they were born in Walterboro or the surrounding area. Were Cy's thoughts leaping to improbable conclusions because of the voice match Rafe had found? Could he rely on such a science to provide answers?

Impatient with himself for wanting to find Kellie's stalker so badly he was starting to cross that line TJ had warned him about, he got up to pace the kitchen. He didn't want to take the time to fix another pot of coffee, so he opted for a soda from the fridge. No sooner had he sat down again than his phone rang. It was ten to three. A check of the caller ID told him it was Jose.

"What's going on?"

"I've got my night-vision goggles trained on a masked figure wearing a dark pullover and pants walking in the alley toward you. Can't tell if it's a man or a woman."

"Don't do anything. Let's see what happens, then close in." He hung up and called to Vic, who sprang off the couch and joined him. "Jose has spotted someone in a mask walking in the alley in this direction."

Vic nodded and drew out his weapon. While he hunkered under the table, where he had a direct view of the doorway, Cy flattened himself against the wall on the other side of the door.

They remained in position ten long minutes before Cy heard the sweet telltale sound of someone picking the lock, probably with a paper clip and tension wrench. If Kellie hadn't gone to the police, the scenario happening to her now would have ended her life. As he geared up for the takedown, a rush such as he'd never known took over.

All of a sudden the door opened. Cy came at the killer from behind and put a headlock on him, forcing him to the floor. The stalker let go with a stream of venom while he fought with the strength of a man high on drugs. Cy felt him bite his arm. It took Vic's help to subdue him long enough to handcuff his hands behind his back and ankle cuff him.

Cy rolled his body over and pulled the mask off his head. There was the face of the man in the picture with the longer hair. He leaned over him. "Surprise, Denny, or whoever the hell you are. Was it Donny, Andy or Drew who strangled the woman in Charleston? I'm the husband you and your twin didn't think existed. You're under arrest for the stalking of Kellie Parrish."

By now Vic was on the phone to the rest of the crew. Within seconds Kellie's town house was filled with agents. Cy took the greatest pleasure in reading him his Miranda rights before he was hauled out to the van.

THE SOUNDS OF men's raised voices had brought Kellie awake. She shot out of bed and dressed quickly in a top and jeans. Cy had told her not to go downstairs. But whatever had been going on below, she couldn't stay up here and not know what was happening. She hurried out of her bedroom and flew down the stairs straight into Cy's arms.

He must have been on his way up to her because he caught her to him, hugging her hard before he held her away from him. "We caught the twin with the longer hair, Kellie. For the sake of practicality, we'll call him Denny. In time we'll catch his brother and you'll never have to be afraid again."

The information he relayed filled her with such relief, she could barely find words. "If anything had happened to you…" Her voice sounded raw.

"Nothing did."

"That's not true. There's blood on your forearm."

"He bit me."

"Let me see." She pushed the sleeve of his shirt up

to his elbow. "You need to go to the ER for stitches and a tetanus shot. You could be infected already."

"The bleeding has stopped. I'll take care of it later. Right now we need to talk." He ushered her over to the couch, where they could sit.

The warmth of his body stayed with her. "I know what you're going to tell me. This isn't over yet."

"No, it isn't." In the soft lamplight, his chiseled jaw stood out in stark relief. "We don't know if his brother was watching what went down here tonight from a distance, or if Denny planned to kidnap you and take you to his brother at another location. What we *do* know is that when the brother we'll call Dan realizes Denny has been arrested or isn't around anymore, his rage will escalate and he'll come after you himself to finish the job. Dan is the one who approached you in Pendleton."

Kellie kneaded her hands. "When he finds out you exist—maybe he believes it now—his hatred toward you is what frightens me."

He gave her arm a squeeze. "Nothing's going to happen to either one of us. Why don't you go upstairs and phone your parents? Tell them that one of the brothers is now in custody, and we're hoping to catch the other one soon. It will be a great relief to them."

"I know." She looked into his eyes. "Are you going to get your arm looked at now?"

"I'll do it after I run by headquarters. Vic will stay here while I'm gone so you'll be safe. I want you to go back to bed and we'll see each other tomorrow."

"It already is tomorrow."

His lips twitched. When he did that, her heart skipped a beat. "So it is."

"Cy?"

"What is it?"

Terrified she might give in to the impulse to kiss him and humiliate herself, she got up from the couch. "Thank you. There should be a better way to tell you how I feel, but I can't think what it is. Please get that arm examined." Before she blubbered all over the place, she left the living room and hurried up the stairs.

She wished she could go with him, but that was ridiculous. He was a Ranger and had business to take care of. He'd just taken down one of the FBI's most wanted criminals. Cy had done his job and needed to finish up.

Kellie sank down on the side of her bed. The trouble was, she'd come to look at him as someone much more than an officer of the law. They'd agreed to a fictional marriage to trap the killers, but tonight she didn't feel like a fictional character.

You'd like to be his real wife. Admit it, Kellie.

Appalled by the admission, and shocked that her feelings could run this deep so quickly, she phoned her parents. They were thankful Cy seemed to have accomplished a miracle so fast, and both were overcome with emotions. After they hung up, she got into bed, hoping she could fall asleep. When the phone rang again, she was surprised to discover it was already seven thirty.

She glanced at the screen on her cell, but there was no accompanying ID.

It was the stalker. He'd left a message. She listened to it.

"You're still lying about having a husband. I saw the police drag my brother out of your garage to their van. You're all going to be so sorry for what you've done. Just wait and see what I've got planned."

He'd been watching the whole time.

She phoned Cy immediately, but it went to his voice mail. She told him about the stalker's message before hanging up.

At this point she was wide-awake. The man who'd invaded her space in Pendleton was still out there, and now it was Cy who wouldn't be safe. Her fear for him was greater than ever.

While she waited for him to call back, she showered and washed her hair. After a quick blow-dry, she put on jeans and a plum-colored cotton sweater. Once she'd pulled on her cowboy boots, she was ready for the day.

As she went downstairs, her phone rang. She checked the caller ID. It was Cy!

With a racing pulse, Kellie clicked on and heard "Good morning."

"The same to you. Did you get any sleep?"

"A little. How about you?"

"Don't worry about me. I heard your message. It means he was hiding behind the fence. Don't leave the town house. I'll be over as soon as I can." She heard the click.

Kellie put the phone on the counter. She needed something to do and started to fix breakfast. In case he hadn't eaten yet, she made enough for both of them. Before long she heard the garage door lifting and ran to open the kitchen door for him.

He levered himself from his car wearing a brown Western shirt and jeans. Kellie had a hard time keeping her eyes off his hard-muscled physique. As he came inside, she could smell his soap from the shower and noticed he was clean shaven. Those deep blue eyes zeroed in on her. His piercing gaze sent warmth through her body. "Something smells good."

Yes, it does. That's you.

"It was my turn to fix breakfast for us. Sit down at the table and I'll serve you."

"I won't say no. I'm starving."

"Since I know you haven't had any sleep in twenty-four hours, you need food to keep you going." She got them started on eggs and bacon, topping it off with toast and coffee.

"This is delicious. Thank you."

"You're welcome. Let me look at the bite on your arm."

He flashed her a lazy smile before rolling up his sleeve. She was relieved to see a dressing had covered it. "I told you I watch out for myself."

"I'm glad you had a doctor look at it."

He rolled the sleeve back down. They were both being polite, but it was like trying to avoid the elephant in the room. He eyed her over the rim of his coffee mug. The gold wedding band on his ring finger gleamed in the overhead light, bringing her straight to the point.

"Cy? We have to talk about our situation."

"Agreed. You go first."

She took a deep breath. "That call this morning made me realize that you and I don't have to pretend to be married any longer. The whole point was to flush out the stalker. Now that he's been arrested and his brother watched what went on—probably from behind the fence—there's no more need for you to stay here.

"Last night my dad said he's going to hire some bodyguards for me as soon as tomorrow. In the meantime I'll let the landlord know I'm moving to my parents' ranch, so my condo will be available for a new renter. That will free you to get on with other Ranger work. We have no idea when the stalker will strike again, let alone when he'll be caught. It could take a long time and you're needed for other important cases."

When Cy didn't say anything, she drank more of her coffee. "It's fortunate that no one knows your name, so no explanations are necessary. After the second brother is arrested, then I'll post the truth about the twin brothers on my blog and explain that the fake marriage was announced to lay a trap that worked brilliantly."

Starting to get unnerved by his silence, she took the rings off her finger and put them on the table. "Take these back to headquarters along with any equipment you've left here. And please thank the other men in your crew for protecting me. They'll never know how grateful I am."

He went on drinking his coffee. Why didn't he say something?

Since they'd finished eating, she got up and cleared the table before putting the dishes in the dishwasher.

"Kellie? If you've said everything you wanted to say, come and sit down while I tell you what I'd prefer to see happen, but it's up to you."

What did he mean? The hairs on her neck started to prickle as she did his bidding.

"I was in a meeting early this morning with the captain. I'm still assigned to your case until it's solved. There's no work more important for the department than for me to put away another killer on the list of America's most wanted. Though we've caught one killer, his twin is on the loose and more dangerous to you than ever.

"Since he knows his brother has been arrested, he's angrier than ever. Until he makes his move, and I expect it will be sooner than later, it'll make my job easier if we stay married so *I* can be your bodyguard. At this point I want us to be visible like any married couple. It will taunt him so much, he'll make a mistake. That's what I'll be waiting for. But if you'd rather your father hired bodyguards who would take turns living here, our department will provide backup. The decision is yours."

Kellie didn't need to think. His suggestion thrilled her so much she could hardly find words. But how to tell him without giving herself away?

"Since you already have a plan, let's not deviate from it now."

She struggled for breath. "Only if you're sure."

"Give me your hand." When she extended her arm, he put the rings in her palm. "Put these back on."

Her heart started to run away with her. Not only because of his touch, but because it meant she wouldn't have to say goodbye to him. Not yet anyway…

"Now, if you don't mind, I'm going to stretch out on the hide-a-bed and get some sleep. To put your mind at ease, Lyle and the crew are outside and will remain on watch until tomorrow."

He got up from the table. "Later today we'll drive out to your parents' ranch and go riding together. I want to watch the famous Kellie Parrish in action. When our stalker phones again, and I know he will, let him leave messages and I'll listen to them later."

And with that, she watched him leave the kitchen, feeling more comforted than ever that her Texas Ranger was here.

Chapter Six

Cy walked into the living room, where he took off his cowboy boots. When he'd proposed that Kellie announce their marriage on her blog, he'd thought she would never agree to it. But she went along with the plan and had her parents' blessing.

Just now he'd assumed she'd put the brakes on this latest strategy. To his astonishment, it didn't happen.

Who knew how long the case might go on. Cy did know exactly how his family was going to react when he told them that he and Kellie were pretending to be man and wife. They were worried he'd never get married and continually tried to line him up with a promising match. The party for his sister coming up on Sunday was another excuse for his parents to introduce him to a new woman.

Because of his undercover role as Kellie's husband, any matchmaking on their part would have to be put on hold. They'd be forced to give up trying to manage his love life while he was still working on her case. Nothing would frustrate them more. Or please him more. In fact he was tempted to take her to the party with him on Sunday.

What was today? Thursday? Was it only last Friday when they'd collided outside the radio station in Bandera? Since she'd come into his world, he'd lost track of time. How could it be that already he couldn't comprehend his life without her?

With a relieved sigh, he stretched out on the bed and turned on his side facing the wall. His body felt as if it weighed a thousand pounds, but the capture of Denny Denham had done a lot to lighten his mood. He could actually go to sleep knowing that when he woke up, he'd be with Kellie, who wasn't going anywhere without him. Later today they'd go riding together. He could hardly wait.

The next time he was cognizant of his surroundings, it was four thirty in the afternoon. He'd been sleeping on his stomach. When he turned over, there she was on the couch across from him, curled up with a book. Their eyes met. Hers were smiling.

Uh-oh. "If I snored, don't tell me about it."

"It will be my secret. But I want to know who Sylvia is."

Cy started to chuckle and sat up. "I don't believe it."

"Believe what?" She smiled broadly, illuminating his world. "It seems you've been carrying around a secret. A little while ago you muttered something like, 'Dammit. Where are you, Sylvia?'"

He couldn't hold back his laughter and moved his pillow so she could see his gun. "*That* is Sylvia."

She put the book down. "You call your gun Sylvia?"

"Yup. She goes everywhere I go, but sometimes when I'm dreaming, I find myself looking for her."

Laughter burst out of Kellie. "You gave it a woman's name. Why not a man's?"

"That's an interesting question. I really don't know."

"Was Sylvia an old girlfriend?"

"No such luck," he teased. "When I was a little boy, my father took me to the barbershop in Dripping Springs for my haircuts. The older man had a picture of his wife, who'd died, on the wall. He called her Sylvia. I guess it stuck in my mind to come out later. Some of my colleagues give their weapons a name."

She nodded. "Just like some pilots name their planes. My grandfather had an old car he called Elvira."

Curious, he asked, "Did you name all your horses?"

Kellie let out a sigh. "No, but one day I'd love it if Trixie gave birth to a little filly I could name and raise."

She could have been talking with the same kind of love she would have for her own baby. He wondered what plans she had for the future. "How long do you intend to compete?"

"After the Finals in December, I'm quitting the circuit. It's a demanding life and I've already been in it so long."

That was news to him. "What will you do?"

"This is a low-cost rental. I've been saving all my earnings and plan to buy a small ranch where I can run my own business of training future barrel racers. I have my eye on several properties that have been put out on the market. That way I can be involved with the rodeo, but on the other end."

He sucked in his breath, marveling over her ambition. "From the amount of fans who flood your website for training tips, I have no doubt you'll be so busy you'll have to turn some away."

"All in good time, I hope."

Enjoying this too much, Cy sat up and pulled on his cowboy boots before he got to his feet. He stared down at her. "Speaking of your website, I happened to look at your schedule before Montana and noticed you competed in rodeos back east."

"Yes. As I told you, Sally's husband, Manny, is a bull rider and we decided to enter those rodeos for points. It was also a fun vacation."

Cy rubbed the side of his jaw. "Since the stalkers were operating in the East, it occurred to me one of them would have seen you perform, possibly in Virginia or more likely in South Carolina. We know Charleston was one of the murder scenes. Since Walterboro is only forty minutes away, I'm thinking he might have gone to that rodeo and decided you were his next victim."

"I had the best time in the ratings that night," she murmured.

"The spotlight was on you. It makes perfect sense. We hope to pinpoint the exact location of their births in one of those two areas. It's possible they maintained a home there."

A delicate frown marred her brows. "To think they might have been following me since January..."

"While Dan tracked you all the way until he showed up in Oregon, his brother broke into the files at the WPRA and obtained your cell-phone number. But remember that there's only one of them now and I'm going to catch him. Excuse me for a minute while I freshen up, then we'll leave for your parents' ranch."

He put the gun in his side-waist holster. After making the bed, he left the living room and went upstairs to the guest bedroom. He shut the door and phoned Vic, who picked up on the second ring. "I wondered when I'd hear from you."

"I was catching up on some sleep."

"Which plan did Kellie go with?" Vic had been in on the meeting with TJ.

Cy stopped pacing. "I gave her a choice."

"And?"

"We're going to carry on as we have been."

"In other words she doesn't want anyone else being her bodyguard. Between you and me, the captain's worried you're going to lose your focus."

His jaw hardened. "Is that what you think, too?"

"It doesn't matter what I think."

"The hell it doesn't!"

"Honestly?" Vic questioned. "I've worked with you for three years and trust you with my life. If you think your plan is the best way to keep her safe and catch this predator, I back you all the way."

"Thanks, Vic. I'm going to need your help."

"You've got it."

"We're leaving for her parents' ranch in a few minutes so she can exercise her horses. The crew will be watching the condo while we're gone."

"While you do that I'm going to see if I can get any information out of our prisoner."

Send For
2 FREE BOOKS
Today!

I accept your offer!

Please send me two free novels and two mystery gifts (gifts worth about $10). I understand that these books are completely free—even the shipping and handling will be paid—and I am under no obligation to purchase anything, ever, as explained on the back of this card.

154/354 HDL GJAE

Please Print

FIRST NAME

LAST NAME

ADDRESS

APT.#   CITY

STATE/PROV.   ZIP/POSTAL CODE

Visit us online at
www.ReaderService.com

"If he talks, it'll be lies."

"Yup. But coming down off his latest fix, he might make a mistake that could be valuable. I'll catch up with you later. Watch your back, Cy."

"Always."

He clicked off and reached for his Stetson.

CY DROVE THEM up to the barn. Kellie got out and headed for the entrance. Cy followed and they walked over to the first stall. "Trixie? I want you to meet a very important person." Kellie's palomino nickered and her ears pointed. "This is Cy. He's going to ride Paladin while we do some circles."

Clearly Cy was no stranger around horses as he rubbed her nose and forelock. "I watched you perform in Bandera, Trixie. You're a champion just like your owner." Her horse nudged him in the chest, causing him to smile at Kellie. When he did that, she forgot where she was or what she was doing.

They moved to the next stall. "This is Paladin, one of Dad's geldings. He's a big bay who loves a good ride. *And* he likes Trixie. When they're out in the pasture, he follows her around."

Cy's eyes gleamed. "I can see why. She's a beauty. Who says romance doesn't exist among our four-legged friends?"

"The only trouble is, he can be annoying and she runs from him."

He burst into that rich male laughter she loved so much. "So she likes her independence."

"At times. But then there are others and she rests her head on his neck."

"Sounds like a mercurial female. I'll do my best to control him."

This close to Cy, darts of awareness shot through her body. Together they picked out their saddles and bridles, then carried them to the stalls. Kellie heard a nicker from another stall.

"Starburst? I haven't forgotten you, but it's not your turn."

A grin broke out on Cy's face. "You talk to them like they're human."

"To tell the truth, I like them better than a lot of humans."

"Amen to that."

Before long they were both mounted. One glance at the gorgeous male astride the bay and she was in danger of melting on the spot. The only way she could describe her condition was that she was in a state of euphoria being with him like this.

He was a natural on a horse and took firm command of Paladin, yet displayed a gentleness that won Kellie's respect and admiration. She decided he could do anything. They rode out to the pasture as if this was something he did every day. Though she hadn't seen him ride in the Bandera parade, she could imagine him with the other three Rangers carrying the flag.

After riding some distance, she headed for the outdoor arena. Cy followed at a slower pace and pulled to a stop. Her pulse raced because he was watching her.

Once inside, Kellie began her routine and made perfect circles with Trixie, always using a little inside leg. She made certain her horse's back feet went in the same track as her front feet. After a few minutes she walked her around, then changed to a trot so she could stand in the stirrups to build up the strength in her legs.

To transition from high speed to stops was part of the routine. So was the exercise of backing up, then calling to her horse to stop. While Kellie was building up her own leg muscles, the exercises were helping Trixie strengthen her hindquarters.

Finally she led her over to the fence and did a few more stops, causing Trixie to use her back hocks and stifles. The routine built the vital control necessary for barrel racing. "Good girl," she called to her horse and patted her neck.

In the background she could hear clapping. When she looked over her shoulder, she saw Cy on Paladin, walking toward them. Beneath his white cowboy hat, his dark blue eyes traveled over her, filling her with warmth. "I wouldn't have missed that expert performance for anything."

"Did you hear that, Trixie? Such high praise coming from one of our famous Texas Rangers." To cover her emotions, she gave her horse another couple of loving pats. "I think you've had a good enough workout for today. It's going to be dark pretty soon. Let's head back to the barn." She glanced at Cy. "I try not to overdo it with her. It's important I make an effort to change her daily routine. Tomorrow I'll work with Starburst for a while."

They rode back in companionable silence. After watering the horses, they put them to bed. On their way out to the car, he asked about her parents.

"They're so thankful you caught one of the stalkers, they decided to attend an important dinner tonight. Otherwise they'd be here to ask you to stay for dinner. But let's go inside anyway to freshen up before we leave for the condo."

In a few minutes they went back to his car. He helped her in and got behind the wheel. "I'm in the mood for a good meal. Have you ever eaten at the Watering Hole? It's only a few miles from here."

He was finally asking her to do something a couple would do, but she couldn't consider this a date in any sense of the word. Cy was hungry and needed to eat. Somehow Kellie had to rein in her thoughts that were growing out of control.

They'd been thrown together because of a life-threatening situation and nothing more. But it was getting harder and harder to remain objective when she was so attracted to him. *It's more than attraction, Kellie. A lot more.*

"I've been there many times," she answered. "Their charbroiled steak is the best in Austin."

"That was easy."

Yes. Way too easy. She was under the Ranger's spell.

Luckily it was the kind of restaurant where you could come as you were. The place was always crowded. While they waited in the lounge area to be called to their table, Anita Wall, one of the women in the Blue Bonnet Posse, made a beeline for Kellie and gave her a hug. "It's so good to see you. I heard you got married. You've got to introduce me."

This was what happened when you went out in public. "Anita Wall? Meet my husband, Cy Vance."

Her married friend and mother looked up at Cy and did a triple take. Kellie couldn't blame her. The man was too striking.

"How do you do?" She shook his hand. "We've all wondered who the man was to snag our star." Her gaze swerved to Kellie before she whispered in her ear, "Now I understand. Wow, wow, wow."

While Kellie tried not to react, Cy asked, "Are you here alone?"

"No. I'm with some friends."

"You're welcome to join us."

She shook her head. "I wouldn't dream of intruding on you honeymooners, but thank you for the invitation." She gave Kellie one more hug. "Call me when you have time to talk."

"I will. It's wonderful to see you, Anita."

To her relief the hostess called their number and Cy escorted her to their table. Once their order was taken, Cy sat back, smiling at her. "Every friend of yours I've met lights up when they see you."

"Every friend of mine can't stop staring when they meet you," she countered before she realized what she'd said. Heat rose to her face. "They'd all be shocked and horrified if they knew what the real reason was for our being together. For your sake I hope the stalker makes another move soon."

"But not for yours?"

She lowered her head. "That came out wrong. Even if this is the career you've chosen, it has to be harrowing for you while you're forced to bide your time waiting for the next opportunity to present itself."

Their food came. Once they were alone again he said, "You have that turned around. You're the one being tortured mentally and emotionally." He cut into his steak. "Some victims would fall apart at a time like this, but not you. Your courage makes my job a lot easier to handle." So saying, he started eating.

"That's because you have a facility for calming me down. It's a gift, Ranger Vance."

Before she broke into grateful tears, she dug into her meal. They ate without talking. When she turned down dessert, he left some bills with the receipt and ushered her out of the restaurant to his car.

As they drove out of the parking lot, she turned to him. "I want to pay you for my share of the dinner. I don't expect the taxpayers of our state to take care of my bill."

"Didn't you notice that I paid cash for our dinner? It's from my paycheck. Any allowance I get as part of the job, I'm issued a credit card for that account. Tonight was my personal treat, if you like."

Kellie liked it too much. "Thank you. That dinner was delicious."

"I agree. Before this case is closed, I might just treat you again."

He got a chuckle out of her.

"That's better. I know you feel like this is the never-ending story, but it will be over before long. Our stalker

Dan is beside himself without his brother. His need to kill again is stronger than ever because they didn't get the job done. In his desperation to finish what they started, he'll reveal himself in some way and that will be his downfall."

"If you say it, then I know it's true."

"I'm touched by your faith in me. How would you like to go to a family party with me on Sunday night?"

The question caught her off guard. "But they'll all think we're married—"

"They know I'm on a case."

"Do your parents realize you're protecting me?"

"Because I'm undercover, they'll figure it out. The point is, my sister is getting married and the parents are inviting a few people over to celebrate the coming event. Because of my job I've been absent from too many family gatherings as it is and would prefer not to miss this one. But I can't leave you alone. Starting tomorrow we won't have backup from the department unless I ask for it. If you don't want to go, we won't."

She bit her lip. "I can see you need a babysitter for me, one armed with a weapon."

"It's all right. Don't give it another thought."

After what he'd just told her? *Ha.* Kellie eyed his arresting profile. "How many sisters do you have?"

"Just Beth, short for Elizabeth."

"Do you have brothers?"

"No. I'm the only one."

"Well, far be it from me to keep you from a party this important. If I had no siblings except one brother,

I know I'd want him there for the most important moment in my life."

Cy looked over at her. "It *is* the biggest thing in her life. I knew I could count on you," he said in a satisfied tone.

Emotional bribery that fed on her guilt went a long way to persuade her. He had no idea how hard this would be on her. They weren't engaged, and she couldn't count on seeing him again after he'd caught the killer. But there was another part of her that was crazy with excitement to go out with him, even if she understood the true reason for being in his company.

They pulled into the garage and he shut off the engine. "Let me have your car keys for a minute." She rummaged in her purse for them. After she handed them to him, he got out and inspected her Toyota, including the trunk. "Okay," he called to her. She started to get out. "But let me go in the condo first."

That was right. While she could forget everything but the joy of being with him, his radar was on alert every second. Kellie waited by the door until he'd turned on lights and told her she could come in. She entered and locked it. They were home for the night, snug and secure.

Despite the menace still lurking out there, she'd never been happier in her life. There was only one reason why, and that reason was walking around, all six foot two of rip-cord-strong Texas Ranger with dark blue eyes and handsome features to die for.

When she thought of Anita and the look on her face

when she saw Cy, Kellie feared it was the same smitten look she'd been walking around with since Bandera.

"Vic brought your laptop back." At the sound of his deep voice, she swung around and saw it on the kitchen table. "The lab has finished with it. Feel free to check your emails and your blog site. Add whatever comes to mind."

The mention of it reminded Kellie of her phone. She'd turned off the ringer. Thank heaven Cy was here. In his presence she wasn't frightened to see who'd called.

After getting it out of her purse, she walked into the living room and sank down on the couch. While Cy was upstairs, she checked her cell. Five messages had been left. One from Cody, who was verifying their trip plans to Rapid City, South Dakota, for the rodeo. She'd call him back. Four came from friends. There was one text message. It came from… *Trixie?*

Kellie felt sick. When she checked it, there was a picture with the text. She pressed on it and saw herself and Cy in his car as they were backing out of her garage. The text read, Plan to say goodbye to your husband, Kellie girl. It'll be payment for my brother. Then I'm going after your horse. Don't forget your turn is coming.

"Cy—" she cried out in panic. Within seconds he came down the stairs. "Look at this! He's a maniac! He's threatening to kill you and my horse!" She handed him her phone so he could see everything.

Without thinking about it, Cy sat down and put his arm around her shoulders to comfort her. He'd been wondering when she'd break down. All this time she'd been so brave, but the threat accompanying the photo of her horse had been the tipping point for her. It was too much. She burrowed into his neck and sobbed.

He brushed the hair away from her cheek. "Awful as this is, it means he's ready to spring into action. But don't worry. Two of the agency's men dressed like local ranch hands are guarding your horses around the clock."

She blinked. "All this time?"

"Yes."

"Oh, thank heaven."

"The stalker doesn't have much more time before you leave for the rodeo next week. I'm convinced he's going to make his move soon. I'll be ready for him," he murmured, pressing kisses to her brow.

One minute she was clinging to him. In the next instant she raised her head to reveal a tear-sodden face. He brushed the moisture from her cheeks with his thumb.

"I—I'm sorry I fell apart like that," she stammered. "How embarrassing."

Cy heard the words, but their lips were only an inch apart, distracting him from his duty to protect her. All that registered was her warmth and beauty, seducing him into wanting a taste of her. It was wrong to give in to his desire, but he'd passed a threshold where chemistry had taken over. He could no more stop what was happening than he could prevent himself from being swept into a vortex.

When his mouth closed over hers, he heard a small moan, then she was giving him access as if she couldn't stop herself, either. For a minute he forgot everything while the wonder of her response had taken hold. One kiss became another and another until it all merged into a growing need that had set them on fire.

He'd never known this kind of ecstasy before, not even with his fiancée. Maybe it was because of the danger surrounding them that the experience of holding and kissing her had surpassed any pleasure he'd known with the few women from his past.

Kellie was exciting from the way she looked, talked, walked, rode a horse and fought her fear. Her smile dazzled him. Her lust for life—her plans for life—thrilled him almost as much as her touch, almost as much as the feel of her body molded to his.

Caught up in a frenzy of giving and taking, Cy unexpectedly heard a familiar voice come into his head. *You realize the two of you will be walking a very thin line.*

Stunned by how far he'd gotten carried away, he lifted his mouth from hers with reluctance. Somehow he managed to let her go and got to his feet. He cleared his throat and stood there with his hands on his hips while he attempted to get his breathing under control. "That wasn't supposed to happen, Kellie. I apologize for betraying your trust, but you have my solemn oath it won't happen again."

She looked up at him through clear blue eyes dominating a flushed face. "It takes two, Ranger Vance. I was right there with you and crossed a line I swore I wouldn't. But I'll tell you this. I enjoyed it."

An honest woman. He smiled, loving her candor. "It was even more exciting for me than watching you round the third can in Bandera and fly straight down the alley."

After running his hands through her hair, Cy could see he'd disheveled it. She smoothed a few strands off her forehead. "It's past my bedtime, so I'll say goodnight."

"I need to keep your phone," he said before she reached for it. Kellie nodded, then stood up and hurried out of the living room.

No sooner had she disappeared up the stairs than Vic called. Cy pulled out his phone and clicked on. "Did you get in to interrogate our prisoner?"

"Yes, but he's not going to give up any information. These guys are real pros, but I have other news you need to see and sent it to your email. I sent the same email to the agents back east who are working on this case."

"How soon can you get here?"

"I'm walking toward the front of Kellie's town house now."

"I'll let you in."

In a few minutes they sat at the kitchen table. Cy handed him Kellie's phone. "Take a look at the message from the sender named Trixie. Dan took a picture of me and Kellie in the car backing out of the garage earlier today."

Vic studied the photo and read the text. He shot Cy a glance. "The loss of his twin has unhinged him."

"Yup. He's starting to take daring risks and is damn good at knowing how to terrorize Kellie. I assume he's armed with a rifle in order to take care of me and Trixie. Then he'll go back to his preferred method to kill Kellie."

"We've got to find him quick."

"Did Janene ever track down that IP address?"

"No. It has her stumped for the moment, but I've received information on the identical-twin birth records from both cities."

"I want to see those, but first let's talk about the photo. Dan was obviously hiding behind the fence this afternoon in order to take it. No doubt he was hidden in the same place when we took his brother out to the van. I'm thinking he's using one of the town houses."

"So am I," Vic broke in. "I'll phone TJ right now to get us a warrant."

They could read each other's minds. "We'll need backup so we can do a thorough search of every town house on this street and the town houses on the other side of the alley. Our lunatic is hiding out here somewhere ready to strike. We need to nab him fast."

"Agreed."

While Vic got on the phone with their captain, Cy opened the email Vic had sent. He studied the statistics for identical twin boys born in hospitals in 1986 when the populations of both areas were smaller. The sum from both cities equaled ten sets, six from Charleston, four from Virginia Beach. Hopefully, the agents at the other end could track down the parents from birth records and make an ID that would help them form a correct profile of the brothers.

Vic ended the call. "TJ's getting the warrant as we speak. He's sending Luckey to guard Kellie so you and I can do the search with the crew. As soon as he gets here, we'll start."

Cy's thoughts were whirling. "I need to tell Kellie

about the change in plans." Since he had her phone, he needed to tell her in person. "Be right back." He got out of the chair and hurried up the stairs with her cell phone.

"Kellie?" he called to her before rapping on her door.

"Yes?" she answered immediately.

"I have to leave for a little while with Vic. But I won't go until Luckey gets here. He's one of my closest friends in the Rangers."

"One of the Sons of the Forty, you mean?"

"Yes. He'll guard you with his life."

"I don't doubt it."

"I'm leaving your phone on the floor outside your door in case you need it. If the stalker calls, let it ring through to your voice mail. I've just put Luckey's phone number in your list of contacts. He'll answer if you call him. Try to go back to sleep if you can, and I'll see you in the morning."

"Be careful, Cy."

He took a deep breath. "Always."

Chapter Seven

I have to leave for a little while with Vic.

Kellie could only imagine what that meant. Instead of lying there shuddering in fear for Cy, she threw back the covers and slid off the bed to get her phone. When she opened her door, she saw her cell but couldn't hear voices downstairs.

Something important was going on and he wanted her out of it, yet he always put her needs first. She believed he was so dedicated, he'd treat any person he was guarding with the same kind of care. That was the problem. Kellie wanted to mean much more to him.

When they'd kissed earlier, she'd never wanted them to stop. She couldn't blame all of it on hormones. This man was different. She was different when she was with him. Kellie had dated a lot of guys over the years, but something had changed when she'd first looked into Cy's startling dark blue eyes.

She picked up her phone and went back into the bedroom. If only there were someone she could talk to about this, but her feelings were too private to divulge even to her family or closest friends. She'd known Cy for only a week. Anyone she confided in would smile and tell her it was natural that a man and woman thrown together in a dangerous situation would grab a little comfort that went along with the hero worship. But in the long run it couldn't be taken seriously.

As she walked over to the bed, more questions ran through her mind. What would it be like to be married to a Texas Ranger? To know that every time he left for work, he was facing danger head-on? When he didn't get home on time, or was involved in a stakeout that kept him away for days at a time, how would she be able to handle it?

Judging by the tension gripping her body right now, she already had the answer to her question. She wouldn't be able to cope. To love Cy meant she would never be at ease when he was out of her sight.

Kellie's mom didn't worry when her husband left the house. She knew he'd walk in at the end of the day and come find her wherever she was. Barring a natural disaster or an unforeseen accident, her mom didn't have to be concerned that she might never see her husband alive again.

Like her mom, Kellie had grown up knowing their husband and father would always be in their lives. She'd never given it a thought. But she did now...

With a tortured sigh, Kellie turned off her phone and lay back, praying this threat to her life would be over soon. If the stalker were caught before she had to leave for South Dakota, she would end her association with Cy cold turkey. That was the only way to deal with her feelings. They never had to see each other again and she could concentrate on getting ready for Finals.

Tomorrow she'd talk to the real-estate agent helping her find the right property to buy. So far she hadn't found the exact thing she wanted. Maybe something else had just been listed on the market. Whether something turned up or not, she'd go on her last four-state circuit of rodeos starting with South Dakota, then Wyoming, Colorado and Oklahoma.

After that she'd come home for three more rodeos in Texas before she left for Las Vegas. Once Finals were over, she'd buy a place to get her new training business started. With the decision made about Cy, she turned on her side. But her mind wouldn't shut off. Being in his arms, being kissed with such hunger, had changed her.

Upset with herself, she turned on the other side. When sleep didn't come, she slid out of bed to get her laptop off the table. The latest scores of her competitors would be listed. Cynthia Lyman from Tombstone, Arizona, was the barrel racer to beat. She'd made the most money for the year, and her last winning time was 13.77.

Kellie needed to do better than that in order to come in first. Her time in Bandera was 14.10. Though she came in second, it wasn't good enough. Once she reached Las Vegas, she'd be competing for ten nights and had to nail those barrels with consistently low scores in the 13s. Focus was everything.

After reading the latest news, she went to her blog. Once she'd thanked people in a general message after reading the latest entries, she posted her schedule of events for the next seven weeks and promised to add to her blog between each rodeo.

Eventually she grew tired and put her laptop on the floor before succumbing to sleep. When morning came, she was surprised to discover she'd slept in until nine. She couldn't remember the last time she'd done that. Emotional exhaustion had to account for it.

Was Cy back?

With her heart in her throat, she showered and dressed in riding clothes and boots. She ran a brush through her hair and put on lipstick before hurrying downstairs.

"Good morning, Ms. Parrish."

Her spirits plummeted to see a dark blond Ranger wearing a polo shirt and jeans seated at the table with his laptop while he drank coffee. He was a close friend of Cy's.

"Good morning. You must be Luckey."

"That's right."

"I take it C—Ranger Vance hasn't come home yet."

"Nope. He's still out working."

She bit her lip. "Have you heard from him?"

"Not yet."

Good grief. What was wrong with her? He wasn't about to discuss Ranger business with her. "I'm going to make breakfast. Would you like some?"

"Sounds good."

"Cy loves bacon and eggs." Cy's name rattled off her tongue. She could have kicked herself for using it.

Luckey's brown eyes smiled. "I think that's an all-around favorite." He didn't miss a thing. Of course he didn't. He was one of the Famous Four she'd heard mention of on the news.

"Good." She got to work and whipped up some biscuits to go with them. Before long they sat across the table from each other while they ate.

"If I'd known that house-sitting Cy's wife was going to come with these perks, I'd volunteer more often."

She shook her head. "Once he catches the stalker, he probably won't be able to live down this fake marriage."

"Cy's a brilliant tactician. That fake marriage caught the first stalker before any of us could blink. It won't be long before he brings the other one into custody. In case you weren't aware, the captain gave the assignment to him because he knew he was the right man for the job."

Kellie knew that already.

"However, I'd like you to know that any of us would have been happy to take your case on after watching you in the Bandera Rodeo."

Luckey was a charmer and very attractive. "You could have no idea how grateful I am for all your help." She got up to pour him another cup of coffee. "I happen to know you were on watch all night long and must be exhausted. If you want to stretch out on the hide-a-bed in the living room, please go ahead while I wash the dishes."

He didn't get up. "If I lie down, then I'll go to sleep. That's a no-no on the job. I'm better off sitting here talking to you."

While she loaded the dishwasher, she asked the first question to pop into her head. "What made you go into law enforcement?"

"I wanted to be a Texas Ranger from the first time I saw a troop of them riding their horses in an Austin parade. I was just a little guy. When I told my dad, he said that we in the Davis family descended from a real Texas Ranger living back in the 1800s. After he showed me my great-great-grandfather's picture, that did it. I was going to be just like him."

"That's a darling story."

His chuckle filled the kitchen.

"Are you married, Luckey?"

"Divorced."

Kellie frowned. "I'm sorry. I shouldn't have asked."

"It's all right. My ex-wife didn't find my occupation darling."

No. She wouldn't. No woman *would* who wanted her husband with her every night of her life. "But if she married you—"

"She thought she could handle it."

With that response, Kellie felt as if someone had just walked over her grave.

He cocked his head. "How come you're not married?"

"I've been too busy chasing a dream."

"And thrilling crowds," he added.

Her mouth broke into a smile. "You're full of it, Ranger Davis."

"I couldn't agree more" came a familiar male voice from the living room. She lifted her eyes in time to see Cy, who walked into the kitchen looking wonderful even though he was tired and needed a shave. How long had he been listening to their conversation? At the sight of him, her heart knocked against her ribs.

She smoothed her palms over her hips. "There's more breakfast if you want some."

"Don't mind if I do." He caught a chair with his boot and sat down by Luckey. If he had any news about the stalker, he wasn't ready to share it with her.

"I didn't know your wife was such a great cook, Cy. Try the biscuits. They're sensational with strawberry jam."

"Yeah?" The two men glanced at each other. Kellie could tell streams of unspoken messages were passing between them.

She poured a cup of coffee for Cy and placed a plate of food in front of him along with utensils. "There's more where this came from."

"Bless you," he murmured, eyeing her with a look that sent coils of heat through her body.

"I'm sure you two have a lot to talk about, so I'm going upstairs. Thank you for watching over me, Ranger Davis."

"It was my pleasure."

Kellie darted out of the kitchen and hurried upstairs. When she reached her room, she fell onto the bed, so relieved Cy was all right she cried tears of happiness into her pillow. Taking a deep breath, she reached for her phone. No call from the stalker. There was only one message. It came from her parents. She should have phoned them last night before she'd gone to sleep.

Without wasting more time, she called them and brought them up-to-date on what was going on. Later in the day she and Cy would drive out to the ranch to exercise the horses. At least that was her plan, but it all depended on him.

"How did the search go?"

Cy looked at Luckey while he ate. "I don't even know where to begin. It curdled my blood when we entered the town house opposite this one on the other side of the fence. According to the landlord, a married couple named Michael and Julie Sanders signed a year's lease in February. When the landlord was shown a picture, he identified Dan as the husband."

"Good grief!"

"No one was home. When we searched the upstairs, we found that the bedroom overlooking Kellie's garage had been made into a shrine. Her pictures were plastered all over the walls and ceiling. Hundreds of them." It had been a nightmarish experience for Cy.

"We found camera equipment and half a dozen guns along with a ton of ammo. One of the rifles has a high-powered scope and was set by the screened window he'd left open. All the weapons are loaded. There's duct tape, pepper spray, handcuffs, ether, everything used in their other murders.

"In the master bedroom Vic found that a part of the closet contained men's clothes. The other half held women's suits and jackets. The upstairs bathroom was filled with makeup and wigs.

"Just yesterday Vic had questioned the owner of a local theater costume shop in town. He remembered selling a lot of women's makeup, including a brown and blond wig, to a man who said he needed them for a play he was producing. When Vic showed him the picture, the owner identified him immediately. The date of the purchase was the first of February."

Luckey shook his head. "That was right before they signed the lease."

"Yup. Those perverts have been holed up there all this time, eying Kellie's every move." Cy hissed the words. "While Denny held down the fort, Dan followed Kellie around the circuit. We found a motorcycle in the garage, so he's out somewhere either on foot or in another vehicle, maybe even a motorcycle."

"No doubt they're responsible for a slug of unsolved armed robberies here in Austin to finance their operation."

Cy's jaw hardened. "We fully expected Dan to walk in on us. When he didn't show up, we left and ordered the other condo renters on both sides of the alley to vacate the premises until further notice. We've organized the crew to stake out his place. After his last phone message to Kellie, my gut tells me he's going to make his move when he gets back from wherever he's been. I'll be his first target. I know how his mind works. He's planning to take me out with the rifle, then he'll break in here for Kellie."

"What do you want me to do?"

"Get some sleep on the hide-a-bed because I'm going to need you later." He got up from the table. "I'll be upstairs catching some sleep myself while I wait for a signal from Kit, who's heading the crew."

"Kit's outside?"

"Yup. TJ wanted the best fresh body to head the stakeout. I told him I wanted Kit. Vic has gone home to get some sleep. After I explain to Kellie what's happening, I'll be in the guest bedroom. She's free to roam around the house, but I don't want her leaving for her parents' ranch today. That will have to wait."

He reached for another tasty biscuit and popped the whole thing into his mouth before taking the stairs two at a time. "Kellie?" Cy knocked on her door.

Before long she opened it. He could see her laptop open, lying on the bed she'd made. She was so beautiful to him, he swallowed hard. When he thought of all the pictures smeared over the walls and ceiling in the other condo, rage for the maniacs who'd been lying in wait for her for almost a year threatened to take over.

"Luckey's asleep downstairs, but we need to talk. Shall we do it in here or in the guest bedroom?"

"Here is fine. Go ahead and use that chair." She walked over to the bed and sat on the side. He brought the chair around so they were facing each other. A quick glance around the room with its piles of soft, colorful pillows on the bed and comfortable accents around the room proved to him a very feminine woman lived inside the cowgirl.

Cy leaned forward with his hands clasped between his legs. "We've tracked down your stalker to his lair. He's not there at the moment. As we speak, a crew from the department has his place surrounded. I don't know how long it will be before he returns. If it extends into days, we'll deal with it. What you need to know is that you're safe as long as you stay in this condo."

She nodded. "I'll phone Dad and ask him to work the horses."

"Good. You're free to move around the condo. I'm going to catch some sleep in the guest bedroom, but I'll be leaving the door open. If there's any activity at all, someone will phone me and Luckey, so you're not to worry about anything. Keep your phone right with you. If the stalker calls, I want you to come and wake me before you answer it. Turn on the speaker and keep him on as long as you can."

"Okay." She stirred restlessly. "I-is he close by?" Her voice was full of fear.

What to say that wouldn't alarm her…? "Yes, but we have everything under control."

"I know that," she whispered and got off the bed to walk around. "What if he has a gun?"

"It won't matter. He'll be surrounded."

Her hands formed fists. "But it *does* matter. Even Texas Rangers with all the protection available have been known to get injured, or worse…"

"That's not going to happen."

Her eyes blazed a hot blue. "He's out to kill you for arresting his brother."

He got to his feet. "I won't give him the chance."

"But if you get shot, it'll be my fault. I couldn't bear it if anything happened to you."

Cy could have sworn that was her heart talking. When he'd agreed to take her case, he'd felt an attraction that had been growing so deep and fast, he didn't recognize himself anymore. TJ had warned him about walking that thin line. Unfortunately he'd already crossed it after meeting her in Bandera and would have pursued her, case or no case.

Get out of her room, Ranger Vance. Now.

"I assure you everything's going to be fine." He put the chair back by the window and left for the other bedroom.

After putting his gun under the pillow, he took off his cowboy boots and lay down, desperately needing a couple hours of sleep. It seemed as if no sooner had his head touched the pillow than he heard a phone ringing. He glimpsed Kellie's face through his eyelids and bolted upright.

She answered the phone and turned on the speaker. "Why do you keep calling me?"

"I like to hear the fear in your voice."

"You like to make people afraid?"

"Why not?"

"That's sick. You're sick, sick, sick!" she yelled into the phone. That brought Luckey from downstairs. Both men listened while she got him going. *Keep it up, Kellie. Stick it to him where it hurts.*

"Does your mother know what kind of person you've turned into?"

Bingo.

"What mother? She didn't want us. We were orphans, but you wouldn't know anything about it with your rich daddy and mommy. You're going to pay for not going out with me. But first I'm going to finish off that husband of yours."

"You don't know who you're dealing with!" Kellie's

lethal tone lifted the hairs off Cy's neck. "Try to hurt him and you'll wish you'd never been born!"

Luckey flashed Cy a secret smile before a maniacal laugh came through the phone. He muttered several obscenities and clicked off.

Kellie looked at Cy. "Did I keep him on long enough?"

"It was perfect. He's ready to explode. That's what I've been waiting for. Let's all go downstairs." He glanced at his watch. To his shock he'd slept seven hours. It was already five thirty in the evening. After putting on his boots, he reached for his gun and followed them out of the room.

"Would you gentlemen like some iced tea?" She'd already gone into the kitchen.

"We'd love it," Luckey answered for them because Cy had made a detour to the living room to phone Kit.

"Any sign of him yet?"

"No."

"He just made another harassing call to Kellie. She pressed his buttons. I think he's going to make something happen as soon as he returns to the town house."

"I'll let you know the minute he shows up. Anything you need and we're ready."

"I owe you for this, Kit."

Cy hung up and walked back in the kitchen. Trust Luckey to get Kellie laughing about something. His friend had a way. "What's so funny?" He'd trained his eyes on her, unable to look anywhere else.

Before she could answer, Cy's phone rang. It was Kit. He turned his back to her. "What's up?"

"The second we got off the phone, a woman with

neck-length brown hair pulled into a stall driving a used blue Sentra sedan. She got out wearing a business suit and heels and has just let herself in the condo."

"We've got him!" Cy blurted with elation. It felt as if he'd been waiting forever for this moment. "He'll be watching from the upstairs window with the rifle. I'll give him ten minutes before I back out of the garage."

"We're on it."

He clicked off and turned to Luckey, who was drinking a glass of iced tea. Kellie was in the background cooking tacos for dinner. "This is it," he muttered. "You know what to do."

"Yup."

Cy hurried upstairs and put on his bulletproof vest. Over it he wore a gray hoodie, and he went back down to the kitchen. "Be sure and save me some dinner."

Kellie's eyes look haunted. "You're leaving now?" He heard the wobble in her voice. "You haven't even drunk your iced tea."

"Sorry. I've got some business to do, but Luckey will enjoy it. Remember he's here to protect you. See you soon."

He opened the kitchen door to the garage and closed it behind him. Once he was in the Subaru SUV, he sat there to synchronize his time to the second with Kit and the crew. He hoped that once he used the remote to open the garage door, the sound would alert the stalker that he was leaving. That was the signal for the crew to move in.

The plan was to back out slowly, giving Dan time to make his best shot.

Five, four, three, two, one.

Up went the garage door. Cy started the engine and let it idle for a minute to draw out the stalker. Then he started backing into the alley. At the point where he turned the car, he braked and shut off the motor. In the split second it took to open the door and roll to the ground, he heard three loud shots fired in succession, shattering the side windows.

Some of the glass grazed his neck and cheek. Moments passed as he stayed down and let the other Rangers do their jobs. Sirens blared as police cars and an ambulance converged in the alley. He got out of the car and saw the street now looked like a war zone. The paramedics ran over to him while he got to his feet and brushed off the bits of glass, but he was waiting for the call from Kit.

When it came, they were the sweetest words he'd ever heard. "Your plan worked perfectly. This stalker was caught in the act. He twisted and screamed while we cuffed him. Now he's on his way to join his twin."

Cy drank in gulps of air. "Thank God."

He couldn't wait to tell Kellie, but he had to ride in the ambulance first while they tended to his wounds, which were superficial. After he'd been taken to the ER, TJ was there to greet him. While Cy sat on the end of the examining table as the doctor put some small bandages over the cuts on his neck and cheek, the captain's eyes played over him with grave concern.

"That was a hell of a thing you did out there tonight, offering yourself up as the sacrifice."

"I was wearing my vest."

"He could have shot your head off."

"I ducked. It was all planned out."

"If you ever try a stunt like that again…"

"You told me this was a high-profile case and you needed it solved ASAP. I just wanted to make sure those two lunatics are put away forever. Trying to take me out added another lifetime sentence to their list of heinous crimes."

After the doctor left the cubicle, the captain said, "I phoned Ms. Parrish and her parents and told them the siege was over. They're probably at her condo right now celebrating."

Cy would have liked to tell her the news himself, but he'd had to follow protocol and get checked over first. "Their relief must be making new people out of them."

His boss nodded. "Thanks to you she's free to live her life fully and win that championship in December. Vic got on the phone to the agents back east. Once again the fame of the Four is going out over the networks for catching two of the vilest criminals wanted by the FBI from coast to coast."

"I'm thinking there may be other murders they've committed. With them both in custody, who knows what information we can get out of them. Hopefully, this will lead to solving some cold cases, too."

TJ flashed him a rare smile. "That's for the detectives to follow up on. What matters is that it took the Texas Rangers to solve this case. Something tells me we'll be hearing from the governor soon. *Again.*" He patted Cy's shoulder. "You've done great work," he said in a quiet voice. "I'm glad you didn't become an attorney."

"Amen," Cy whispered. Otherwise he would never have met Kellie. "Don't forget it took the whole team, TJ. But thanks for going along with my unorthodox plan. I believe that was the word you used."

"You flushed them out with your clever sting in record time. According to your buddies, this marriage seems to have agreed with you. What do *you* say?"

"The jury is out where that's concerned."

He nodded. "Vic's waiting in the lounge. When you're ready, he's going to drive you home. Take the day off tomorrow to recover before you write up all the details of the case. That's an order."

"Yes, sir."

After the captain left, Cy got off the table and reached for his hoodie and vest. He found Vic and they walked out to his friend's car. "I appreciate the lift home."

En route to Cy's house, Vic glanced at him several times. "The captain was right. You're damn lucky to have walked away from that shooting."

"If you're going to tell me you wouldn't have done the same thing, I wouldn't believe you. After Dan made his last harassing call to Kellie earlier today, I knew I was his next target. Which means the best move was to play it out on my own terms. While he was concentrated on me, the crew closed in, taking him by surprise."

They grabbed some burgers at a local drive-through, then headed for Vic's house in South Austin. Cy had chosen to live in a secluded neighborhood hidden away in a wooded area. His rustic lodge-style home with exposed wood appealed to him for several reasons. Besides a loft where he had his office, the open floor plan was dominated by a cathedral ceiling with tons of natural light.

When they reached the entrance, it dawned on him he hadn't stepped foot in his three-bedroom house for over a week. Normally after being away on a case, home sounded good to him while he relaxed. But tonight he knew something was missing even before he got out of the car. He knew what it was. Kellie wouldn't be here when he walked inside.

Over the past seven days, they'd spent hours together. When they had to be apart, she'd been constantly on his mind. If it weren't so late, he'd drive over to her town house right now with the excuse that he wanted to collect anything he'd left while working the case.

But before that, he needed a shower and a shave.

Vic turned to him. "You look like death. Go to bed and we'll talk in the morning."

Cy opened the door. "I couldn't have done this without you. I owe you big-time."

"I'll remember that when the captain gives me my next case."

"Good night, Vic." He shut the door and went in the house carrying his vest and pullover. Without turning on lights, he climbed the stairs to his bedroom in the loft located across from his office. He plunked his things in the chair and moved over to the bed to pull off his boots.

The moonlight coming through the window caused the gold band on his ring finger to gleam. He needed to remove it before he went into headquarters in the morning. The boss had told him to take the day off. For the first time since joining the Rangers, the thought of nothing to do all day long sounded like a death sentence.

A whole day without Kellie? He wouldn't know what to do with himself. The captain's question went round in his head.

According to your buddies, this marriage seems to have agreed with you. What do you say?

Cy threw back his head, afraid to answer it out loud. If he did that, it would be tantamount to a confession that could change his whole life. Especially if Kellie didn't answer it the same way.

Chapter Eight

Ten after midnight. No phone call from Cy. No door-bell ringing.

Kellie's parents had left her town house at ten thirty. They'd begged her to go home with them, but she'd told them she was exhausted. After the exciting phone call from the captain of the Rangers, who praised Cy's hero-ism for leading the team that caught both stalkers, she preferred to go straight to bed. She would drive out to the ranch in the morning.

Luckey had stayed with her until her parents arrived. He'd received a call from one of the other Rangers let-ting him know Cy had been taken to the hospital but his injuries were minimal.

She didn't believe that for a minute, and the fact that he hadn't tried to make contact convinced her some-thing was seriously wrong. She'd heard the shots and learned what had happened from Cy's superior. But he was trained to gloss over information he didn't want her to know. Luckey had prevented her from going out in back while it was still a crime scene. She recognized he was only doing his job, but it killed her that she had to wait for information that came in bits and pieces.

That was the part of the exclusive Ranger brotherhood that bothered her. Surely Cy had to know she was anxious to hear his voice and make sure he was all right, even if she couldn't see him.

Restless and worried, Kellie paced the floor and then sank down on the couch. Cy's hide-a-bed was still in the living room. He would have to come back to get it, but obviously not tonight.

She glanced down at the rings. He'd be taking those back, too. But she felt as if they'd become a part of her. She would sleep wearing them one last time.

At one in the morning, she took some ibuprofen for a headache and went upstairs to bed. The painkiller helped her to fall asleep, but when she awakened Saturday morning, she realized she'd been crying. She'd had nightmares.

Because of her ordeal, her parents had worried she wouldn't sleep well and might have bad dreams. But oddly enough, it wasn't the stalkers who had filled her mind. Throughout the night she'd wandered endlessly in her search for Cy, unable to find him anywhere.

Thankful to be awake, she got out of bed to shower and wash her hair. If Cy came over this morning, she wanted to be ready for him. After putting on a clean pair of jeans and a plaid Western shirt, she applied some makeup and pulled on her cowboy boots before going downstairs.

While she was in the kitchen pouring herself a glass

of orange juice, her phone rang. Fighting her disappointment that it wasn't Cy, she reached for it. "Mom?"

"Honey? Turn on the news. We'll talk after it's over."

Taking her juice with her, she hurried into the living room and turned on the TV to one of the local stations. Between swallows she watched the breaking news.

"For those of you who've just joined us, last evening our own Texas Rangers finished up a sting that ended in the arrest of two killers on the FBI's most wanted list. Three brutal unsolved murders stretching from Illinois to Tennessee and South Carolina might have turned into four if it hadn't been for our state's bravest. We're standing by for a message from the governor."

Kellie sank down on the couch to listen.

"Today is one of the finest days for the Rangers, who prevented the murder of one of our celebrated Austin citizens, Kellie Parrish. She's the twenty-five-year-old barrel racer who will be competing in the National Finals in Las Vegas in December. She has been stalked by identical twin brothers whose killing spree started four years ago.

"The same rangers who brought down the drug cartel here six months ago took the lead in the capture of these predators. The criminals' names are being withheld as FBI agents in Illinois, Tennessee and South Carolina are putting all the facts together and notifying family members of the women they'd targeted."

A shiver ran through Kellie. The thought of the poor parents and families of the three women who'd been terrorized and killed brought stabbing pain to her heart. Because of Cy, they could now be provided with answers. But those poor women hadn't been blessed to have Cy protecting them.

Without wasting a breath, she phoned her mother. The minute she heard her voice, she broke down sobbing. "Oh, Mom. Cy is so wonderful." She tried to hold back the sobs, but it was pointless. "I don't want to think what would have happened if he hadn't taken my case."

"Then don't, darling. Have you talked to him since last night?"

"No. He had to go to the hospital last night. Maybe he's still there. I have no idea how serious his injuries were. Even if he's been released, I'm sure he has so much to do."

"I don't wonder. How soon are you coming?"

She wiped her eyes with her other arm and took a fortifying breath. "I—I don't know yet."

"Sitting around waiting to hear from him isn't the answer."

Kellie jumped to her feet, hurt by her comment. "What do you mean?"

"The two of you have been living in close quarters throughout your ordeal, pretending to be married. Now that the threat has gone, I'm not at all surprised you miss having him at your side on a constant basis. He's the stuff heroes are made of. Heavens, I'm a little in love with him myself. Please don't tell your father."

"Oh, Mom." She let out a half laugh because her mother knew her so well.

"I'm not surprised you've lost your head, but you've got a championship to win, remember? Ranger Vance isn't going anywhere. Give it time."

Kellie hated it when her mother was right.

"Thanks for the talk. I should be at the ranch within the hour."

After she got off the phone, her mood was completely different. She rushed upstairs for her purse and came back down to write a note at the kitchen table.

Dear Cy,
Words can't express what I'm feeling, so I'm not going to try. I forgive you if you let yourself in to get the rest of your things while I'm not here. The governor gave you a ringing endorsement today. Congratulations. Just know that you will always have my undying gratitude. You saved my life. What greater service can one human do for another?
Kellie

She read it over several times, wondering if she needed to change anything. But no, it said what she wanted to say. Unlike the piece she'd written on the blog about their marriage, this one wasn't over-the-top. Viewing it objectively, she felt she'd hit just the right tone.

Without giving herself a chance to change her mind, she removed the rings and left them on top of the note. After grabbing the extra garage-door opener from the drawer, she hurried out to the garage and climbed in her car.

When she backed out, she saw no sign of the crime scene from last night. But it·was out here that the stalker had fired on Cy. Another shudder left her weak before she pulled herself together and started for the ranch.

During the drive, half a dozen messages were left on her phone. She knew she would be inundated by good wishes and concern from her friends for a while, but she wasn't ready to talk to anyone about this except her parents. Then she would take separate rides on Trixie and Starburst, exactly what she needed to sort out her head.

Her left hand gripped the steering wheel. It looked bare without the rings. *How do they feel, Mrs. Vance?* he'd asked, staring at her with his gorgeous dark blue eyes.

They'd felt natural.

Without them, without him, nothing felt natural.

Another two miles and she pulled up in front of the ranch house. Her phone rang again. She glanced at the caller ID and rushed to answer it. "Cy?"

If he hadn't known how she really felt about him, he did now.

"Good morning, Kellie."

He sounded wonderfully alive. She gripped the phone tighter. "Are you still in the hospital?"

"I'm at headquarters. Last night I was only there for a few minutes to have a couple of tiny cuts treated before going home."

"I'm so thankful you weren't seriously injured." Her voice shook. "I heard three shots."

"It's over now." It was obvious he didn't want to talk about it. "If you're still at your town house, I'd like to come over and get my stuff. Vic's coming with me.

We'll take out the hide-a-bed so you can have your house back."

Kellie moaned. If she hadn't left so soon…

"I'm sorry, Cy. I'm out at my parents' house. You still have a door key, right?"

"Yes."

"I can imagine how busy you must be, so feel free to drive over and let yourself in."

After a slight pause, he said, "Sounds good. I'll leave the key and your garage-door opener on the table."

Her eyes closed tightly. She'd purposely left the rings and the note in case something like this happened. "Cy? I want to see you again to thank you. Is there a night you could come over and I'll cook dinner for you?"

"You don't need to do that."

"There's every need. You saved my life."

"Tell you what. The captain has a new case for me. I need to take a look at it. When I know my schedule, I'll call to let you know what night would be good."

So now that he didn't have to guard her, he wasn't planning on taking her to his sister's engagement party on Sunday evening. Already he'd been put to work on another dangerous assignment. That was his job.

For one week out of her life, the two of them had been inseparable. But it was over. He'd never again be exclusively hers. How was she going to bear it?

"I hope you can make it Monday or Tuesday. Cody and I will be leaving for South Dakota on Wednesday."

Another silence before he said, "How long will you be gone?"

The breath froze in her lungs. "Seven weeks."

"Seven?" He sounded surprised. "Without a break?"

"After I leave Oklahoma I'm doing three rodeos throughout Texas with Sally and Manny. It'll be November before I return home." She stared blindly into space waiting for a response.

"If I can't make it either of those nights, will you give me a rain check?"

Kellie had to brace herself to handle the hurt. "Do you even have to ask? Ranger Vance will always have a standing invitation to my home."

"That's nice to hear."

She could hardly swallow. "I'm so glad you're all right. Take care of yourself, Cy. The Famous Four wouldn't be the same without you."

Enveloped in pain, Kellie clicked off before she said too much. Then she turned off her cell. She was glad he hadn't learned she was still at the condo earlier waiting around for him.

The remark her mother had made during their phone call had gotten her out of the house in time to save her from making the biggest mistake of her life!

CY PULLED THE van in front of Kellie's town house with a grimace. "Let's get this done fast." He didn't wait for Vic. After he got out and opened the side door to accommodate the hide-a-bed, he headed for her front door. The key was on his ring.

Vic followed him inside. They made quick work of getting the couch out to the van. In a few minutes he'd restored the living room to its former order. "I'll run upstairs to grab my laptop and any clothes I left."

"While you do that, I'll take down the camera from the garage."

"Good. Be back in a second."

When he came down with his bag, he went into the bathroom to pack the toiletries he'd left. All was done except to leave the key and garage-door opener.

Cy walked into the kitchen and put both items on the table. That was when his eyes were drawn to the diamond and wedding band he'd given her. They were sitting on a note she'd penned. A vise seemed to close around his chest.

He pocketed the rings before reading it. The last lines stood out. *Just know that you will always have my undying gratitude. You saved my life. What greater service can one human do for another?*

Kellie had written this before he'd phoned her. Now that the threat to her life was over, she hadn't been able to remove the rings fast enough. She hadn't mentioned tomorrow night's party, not even a hint that she still wanted to go with him.

So what in the hell did those kisses mean the other night when they'd both come close to losing control? Gratitude had nothing to do with the way she'd melted in his arms, kissing him until he felt immortal. She'd been on fire for him. That wasn't something you could hide.

Vic joined him. "What's going on, Cy? You haven't been the same since you walked into headquarters this morning. If I didn't know better I'd say you've seen a ghost."

Cy lifted his head. "TJ was right. He warned me

that pretending to be married meant I'd be walking a very thin line. At the time I didn't realize how much truth he spoke." *Or how much I wanted it to be real.* He turned to his friend. "That's why *he's* the captain. Let's get out of here."

He walked out of the house, making sure the front door was locked before he closed it. When they got in the van, Vic turned to him. "Come on, Cy. It's me you're talking to. Something's eating you alive. What is it?"

Cy tossed his head back. "I think I've been played."

"By whom?"

"Who do you think?"

"You couldn't mean Kellie."

"Until I read her note, I didn't think it was possible, either. Gratitude is the last thing I want from her."

Vic cocked his head. "I take it you two crossed the line."

"Only one time. After Dan threatened to kill her horse, she fell apart and I comforted her. Things got out of control for a few minutes. That's all."

"Apparently it was enough to turn you inside out."

"Never again," he vowed through gritted teeth.

"Listen to me, Cy. You're too close to the situation and not thinking straight. Try looking at this from her point of view. Before my wife died, I learned a lot from living with her. Not everything is what it seems to be. Kellie had to have feelings for you or she wouldn't have kissed you. But don't be upset because she's grateful to you for saving her life. Both emotions can coexist in the same universe."

He took a sharp intake of breath. "You saw the wedding rings on the table."

"Now that I think about it, I see you're not wearing your wedding band, either. How come?"

"You know damn well why."

"Can't you believe she took her rings off for the same reason?"

"But did she?"

"Only you can answer that question. Has she left you with no hope?"

Cy rubbed his eyes. "It's not like that. She said she wanted to cook dinner for me. I knew it was just her gratitude talking. But the other night I told her my sister's engagement party is on Sunday night. Since I didn't dare leave Kellie alone, I asked her if she'd be willing to go with me and she said yes. But now that the case has been solved, she didn't—"

"Didn't what?" Vic challenged. "Tell you she still wanted to go with you?"

"No," Cy muttered.

"Did you ask her if she still wanted to go? Maybe she was waiting for you to bring it up. You've been joined at the hip for a week in the most dangerous kind of situation, but now that you no longer have to pretend you're married, I'd say she's feeling a damn sight vulnerable... and probably nervous."

He flung his head around. "Nervous—of me?"

"You've been in charge all this time, dictating every move. Maybe she fears *she's* been played."

"Hell—"

"Yup. And hell is where you're going to stay till you get this thing straightened out."

Stirred up by Vic's perceptive comments, he started the engine and they took off for the warehouse at head-quarters. Once they'd dropped things off, Vic left for home while Cy walked through to his office.

Hell wasn't the place he wanted to be. He sat down at his desk and phoned Kellie. No doubt she was out riding and it would probably go through to her voice mail. If so, he'd wait until he got a live response, even if it took until he went to bed.

In the meantime he opened the file folder on the new case TJ had given him.

Fidel Ravelo is wanted in connection with the armed robbery of approximately $7 million from a security company in North Austin, Texas, that took place two years ago. He allegedly took three security employees hostage at gunpoint and handcuffed, bound and injected them with an unknown, nonlethal substance to disable them further. The FBI is offering a reward of up to $1,000,000 for information leading to Ravelo's capture. He's believed to be in Venezuela, but re-cent rumors say he's been seen in Brownsville, where he has ties to family.

After studying the specifics, he'd start by talking to the security employees. Maybe one of them could recall a detail that hadn't been included in the report. But he couldn't do any more work today. The captain had told him to go home. Cy decided to take his advice because he could no longer concentrate.

KELLIE FINISHED SHAMPOOING Trixie and rinsed her off. After putting a little conditioner on her tail and mane, she brushed them to make them silky. Her last action was to use a damp cloth to rub her palomino's face. Then she gave her a kiss and some Uncle Jimmy's Squeezy Buns for a treat. She and Starburst chomped them down.

"There! Now you two look beautiful and I'm sure you feel much better." Both horses stood in the late-afternoon sun while she towel-dried them so they wouldn't catch cold. On Monday the vet would come out to look them over and check their hooves before the trip to South Dakota.

"All right, girls. It's time for dinner." She grasped their lead ropes and walked them to their stalls inside the barn. After removing their bath halters, they could eat from the hay nets and drink water.

The exercise had been good for her, reminding her these horses were her children and her passport to a championship. "See you tomorrow."

She could hear nickering and walked to Paladin's stall. Only two days ago Cy had ridden him. The memory of that heavenly afternoon made her ache for him. "You want a treat, too?" Kellie fed him the last of her horsey treats and walked out to clean up the grooming equipment. Once she'd coiled the hose, she headed back to the ranch house.

Today she'd wondered if she would make it through

to evening without Cy, but here she was still walking around. And thanks to him, still alive. Somehow she had to get beyond all this. Earlier in the day her father had told her this was a time for debriefing. By working with her horses, it would help put the horror of her experience behind her. The passage of time would do the rest, but she couldn't hurry the process.

Her mind thought about Cy. Every time he solved a case for the agency, how did he put the horror behind *him*?

She let out an anguished sigh. When she looked to the sun getting ready to set, she noticed the sky was shot through with pinks and yellows. The same sky Cy might be looking at tonight. How long would it take her to stop missing him? Was he missing her right now? Had the magic between them been a figment of her imagination? Those moments in his arms were real enough.

If he were her husband, how would she deal with their separations, knowing that every time he left the house it was possible he might not come back? Under those conditions, how long could the magic last?

"Not very long," she whispered to the air. Kellie didn't have the right stuff to live with a hero like Cy. That was what he was. It took a special type of woman who could compartmentalize her feelings in order to deal with that kind of stress on a day-to-day basis.

Once she reached the ranch house, she went upstairs to her old bedroom to shower. Since she had no appetite, she got ready for bed and reached for her laptop. It was time to draft a disclaimer to put on her blog. She'd known this day would have to come. Who knew Cy would solve her case this fast?

Kellie got to work on it. When she'd finished, she read it over half a dozen times, but she needed another opinion before posting it. Since it was only eight thirty, she reached for her cell phone to call her friend Kathie. Seven messages were waiting for her, including one from Kathie. It wasn't until now she remembered that she'd turned off her phone. The last one was from Cy. He'd called hours ago. She couldn't believe it.

Her hand trembled as she pressed the button and listened. "Kellie? Call me ASAP."

The urgency in his deep voice gave her heart the greatest workout of its life. He'd solved her case and was already working on another one. Why was he calling her now? Had he left something at the town house he'd forgotten and didn't want to be accused of breaking in to get it?

If she didn't phone him back, she'd never know the answer to that question. His call gave her the excuse to talk to him again. Feeling light-headed from emotions bombarding her body, she pressed the digit for his number.

He picked up on the second ring. "Kellie?"

"Hi." She was trying to catch her breath.

"Thanks for calling me back."

"I didn't know you'd phoned until a minute ago. I've been out shampooing my horses and just finished."

"How lucky for them."

She chuckled in spite of her angst. "They love it and they were so good for me. They didn't move."

"That doesn't surprise me. They love you. Horses aren't that different from humans. Rosco P. likes to do tricks for me."

"Rosco P.?" Kellie was charmed down to her toenails by the revelation. "Was he the horse you rode in the Bandera parade?"

"That's right."

"I didn't know that was his name. Sounds like the bumbling character from the old *Dukes of Hazzard* television show with Boss Hogg."

"The very one."

"I adored that series. The way those brothers drove that car around, driving the Boss crazy, was hilarious."

"I got a kick out of it, too."

"What kind of tricks can you get your horse to do?"

"He can bow and do the Spanish walk."

"You're kidding!"

"Nope. Most of the time I use a ball to play with him. For incentive I feed him Rounders Molasses treats."

"Starburst likes those, too." Kellie almost said that they'd have to get their horses together, but she stopped herself in time. "Cy—I'm probably keeping you from your work. Did you forget something at the town house? Is that why you called me?"

"No. I phoned to ask if you want to go to my sister's engagement party tomorrow night. We'd talked about it before, but that was when I was protecting you. Now that the threat is over, we can go without worrying about our undercover lie."

She pressed a hand to her mouth to stifle a cry of joy. He still wanted her to go with him.

"I'd like that very much."

"If it works for you, I'll pick you up at your town house at six thirty. It's a semidressy affair."

"Thanks for telling me. I live in cowboy boots and forget they're not suitable for every occasion."

"Understood. I know you have questions about how everything went down last night. I'll do my best to answer them. See you tomorrow night. I look forward to being with you again, Kellie."

Her pulse raced. "Me, too. And you're right. I'd like a little closure. Good night." *I want to see how serious your injuries are.* She hung up in a daze, suddenly motivated because she knew she'd be with Cy tomorrow night.

In the morning she'd clean her one-stall horse trailer and living quarters to get it ready for her trip around the circuit. Kellie had to put fresh feed and hay on board, plus all her gear and plastic barrels.

She had nine or ten different bits and took them with her along with several pairs of reins and halters. In her dressage training routine she felt snaffles were the best, plus the square mouthpiece O-ring, so her horse's mouth would stay soft and undamaged.

Once the vet came out to check her horses, she and Cody would be ready to go. He and his fiancée would be over on Wednesday to load Starburst and they'd all drive in tandem. What she'd give if Cy were in a different line of work and could travel to the various rodeos with her.

You're crazy, Kellie.

One phone call from him and her head was in the

clouds again. She couldn't afford to forget what he did for a living. He'd dodged a bullet while protecting her, but what about his next case, and the one after that?

By the time she'd given herself another talking-to, a great deal of her excitement had dissipated. A night out with Cy would be wonderful, but she'd pay a price. She just knew it! But it was too late to cancel on him, and she didn't want to.

After turning out the light, she crawled under the covers with her mind made up that it would be their final goodbye.

Before she left for South Dakota she'd post her blog piece. But Kathie deserved an explanation over the phone first. She'd been hurt that Kellie hadn't told her about her marriage. That was something she could fix right now.

Kellie hadn't really been in touch with anyone since the stalker first approached her in Oregon. Cy had made up her whole world and still did.

Knowing she wouldn't fall asleep for a long time, she reached for her cell. While they were on the phone, she could run the blog piece by her friend and see if she had any other suggestions before it went out. When Kellie thought about telling everyone she really hadn't gotten married, she felt so hollow inside, she could hardly stand it.

By six on Sunday evening, Kellie had showered and shampooed her hair. There was enough natural curl that she blow-dried it into a wavy bob with a side part.

Once she'd applied her lipstick in a tangerine frost color she loved, it was time to get dressed.

She had several outfits, but in the end she chose her sleeveless black flared jersey dress with the high rounded neck. Her tiny black-and-gold puffed teardrop earrings went perfectly with it. On her feet she wore black sling-back high heels. Before she left the bedroom, she reached for her black clutch with the gold fastener.

One last look in the mirror and she realized she didn't need any blusher. The temperature she was running did it for her. Kellie would be meeting Cy's family tonight. She needed to look her best for him.

At twenty after six the doorbell rang. Her heart leaped because he was early. She hurried downstairs to let him in. How ironic that only two days ago, Cy had permission to come and go as if he lived here while he carried out his plans to protect her.

When she opened the door, the tall, spectacular-looking male in the midnight-blue suit and lighter blue shirt almost caused her legs to buckle. Kellie had to hang on to the door handle or she would have fallen. She noticed a small bandage on the side of his neck above the collar, but nothing else, thank heaven. He was here—and he was okay.

Chapter Nine

Cy took in the vision before him. Mounted on her palomino, Kellie Parrish in Western attire was a complete knockout. But tonight the champion barrel racer had taken on a different persona. To say she was dazzling in black was an understatement.

She had a glow about her he hadn't seen before now. The stalker brothers had stolen that radiance from her, but now that they'd been caught, she'd been restored to her former self. Her heart was in those blue eyes, and she was looking at him the way she'd done when they'd kissed each other senseless the other night.

"Hi" was all he could say until his breathing returned to normal.

"Hi," she answered in a soft voice. "I'm ready."

"Make sure both doors are locked."

It brought a smile to her face. "I did."

"Sorry. Old habits die hard."

"I forgive you," she murmured as he walked her to his Audi sports car parked in front of the town house. Once he'd started the engine and they were off, she turned to him. "How long will it take us to get to Dripping Springs?"

"That depends."

"On what?"

"Maybe we'll just drive into the sunset. What would you say to that?"

The blood pounded in her ears. *I'd go anywhere with you.* "I'm not sure your sister would forgive you."

"What if I told you I'm tired of doing my duty?"

He felt her glance. "Your sister isn't a duty."

"True. But the way you're looking tonight, I'm not sure I want to share you with my family. You look stunning, Kellie."

"Thank you," she whispered. "You look better than I feared you would after being sent to the hospital."

He thought he heard a compliment in there somewhere. "I had no choice but to go in the ambulance. Those were the captain's orders. Otherwise I would have come back in the town house to talk to you."

She nodded. "Luckey told me as much."

"Well, Ms. Parrish—we have a half hour of privacy before we reach my parents' home, where you'll be bombarded with questions. Ask me anything you want."

"I want to know how you knew the stalker would come after you in the alley."

"When I realized the stalker had a clear look at your garage in order to take that picture, and to see his brother hauled out to the van in the very same place, I decided he could be hiding out in one of the town houses on either side of the alley. So Vic and I went door to door. We hit the jackpot when we entered the town house opposite yours through the fence. Those two criminals had been renting it since February."

He heard her gasp. "I don't believe it. All this time?"

"We found enough evidence inside to help the agents in winding up the other murder cases back east." Cy didn't tell her about the shrine. It would horrify her, and she didn't need the added trauma now that they'd been incarcerated. "Dan kept a loaded rifle with a scope by the side of the bedroom window overlooking your garage.

"After he sent you that last phone message about getting rid of your husband, I decided to draw him out. When the team saw Dan return to the town house dressed like a woman, I figured he would make his move against me soon. So I set it up and hoped he'd hear the garage door open. If he hadn't done it when he did, then he would have tried again and again. It was my luck that he was so angry, he took the first chance he got.

"I backed the car out. As soon as I turned the wheels, I knew he'd take a shot if he was going to, so I stopped the car and rolled out to the ground. Those three shots shattered the glass. That was it. The team closed in on Dan, who had no idea they were staking him out, and took him away."

She lowered her head. "You could have been killed so easily."

"No. The setup was on my terms. I knew what I was doing. Those evil twins are going to be sent to prison for life without parole."

"The governor praised you on TV."

"It was all in a day's work."

"Don't be absurd, Cy. What you did was as great as what the Original Forty did when they saved Texas."

"That comparison is way over-the-top. Just remember that saving you was greater, and I couldn't have done it alone."

"But it was all your brainchild. Sometimes you seem bigger than life. I'm in awe of you."

Cy smiled to himself. He'd take that for a start. "It helped that the target of those killers happened to be a woman who's the pride of Texas. You showed courage under fire and stayed in control while they terrorized you. Kind of like the way you handle Trixie when you race into the arena. Thousands of rodeo fans across the country are in awe of you."

"You're never going to let me thank you properly, are you?"

They were driving into Dripping Springs. Cy took the first turnoff and drove to a neighborhood park with a small lake. After pulling to a stop in an area away from other people, he stopped the engine. He undid his seat belt and turned to her, sliding his arm along the back of her seat. "What is your definition of *proper*?"

He waited while she digested his question, then she undid her seat belt. His heart thudded as she launched herself at him, throwing her arms around his neck. She started kissing his face. Every feature. *"This and this and this!"*

Suddenly her mouth reached his and he forgot everything except the thrill of holding her in his arms once more. She was no longer the woman he had to protect. For the first time, he was free to kiss her and show her what she meant to him without having to hold back his passion. He'd been aching for her since they'd kissed a few days ago.

"I've missed you for the last two nights," he whispered into her shimmering hair. Her fragrance enveloped him.

"It's been hard since you moved out," she admitted. "I know we were only together for a week, but I got used to being with you. To be honest, I feel lost."

"I know the feeling." Cy crushed her mouth again, never wanting this ecstasy to stop. They couldn't get close enough. He would never be able to get enough of her.

"We're going to be late for the party," she struggled to say after he lifted his mouth so she could breathe.

He groaned. "What party?"

"The one I got dressed up for."

"I guess we have to go so I can show you off."

"Does your family know you're coming?"

"I texted them I'd be there."

"Do they know you're bringing someone?"

He cupped her beautiful face in his hands and kissed her thoroughly. "No. It will be fun to surprise them. That is if we make it there."

They gave in to their desires once more before Kellie pulled away from him. "You *have* to go." She moved to her side of the car and fastened her seat belt.

Resigned for the moment that this would have to wait until later, he got the car going and they drove the rest of the way to his parents' home in silence. Before they pulled in the driveway, he saw a dozen cars parked on both sides of the street. Hurricane lanterns with lighted candles lined the walkway to the front door of the spacious rambler.

"Since the wedding and reception will be held at the church, my folks have gone all out for this party." He turned off the car.

"I'm not surprised. Your sister is their only daughter."

"Beth has been doted on. She came along when my parents didn't think they could have another child."

"My parents had to wait a long time before they got me. How old is she?"

"Twenty-three. She has her degree in English. After New Year's, she'll be teaching at a middle school." He got out of the car and went around to help her out. "I'll tell you a secret. She's afraid of horses. Always has been."

Kellie looked up at him in surprise. "Was she hurt by one?"

"No. But she fell off her mount during a ride when she was little. My dad tried to help her overcome her fear, but she wouldn't do it. After that experience the only time she'd try it was if Dad or I took her on rides on our horses."

"Oh… What a shame. Does her fiancé ride?"

"He tolerates it if he has to."

She smiled. "Can you imagine having to tolerate Rosco P.?"

"No." Kellie was so lovely he lowered his head to kiss her mouth once more. "She and Tom are a good match," he whispered against her lips before he walked her to the front door and let them into the foyer.

"Well, look who's here—"

Cy might have known his father's older brother would spot them first. "Your mom said you were coming. We've all been waiting for the man whose name has been in the news for the second time this year. Well done, Cy." He gave him a pat on the shoulder before his glance fell on Kellie.

"Uncle Bruce? Allow me to introduce Kellie Parrish. She's—"

"All of Texas knows who she is." His uncle shook her hand, eyeing her in admiration. "It's an honor to meet our state's leading rodeo champion." He looked back at Cy. "And *your* wife, I understand. You always were a dark horse."

"No—" Kellie blurted, darting Cy an anxious glance. *Hell.* "How many people know about that?"

"Everyone at the party." His uncle smiled at Kellie. "My son's wife, Terrie, reads your blog religiously, and the word spread. Come with me. We're all waiting to meet the two celebrities of the evening."

"I'll handle this," Cy whispered to her and put a hand on her back as they walked into the living room. All the chatting ceased, then everyone started clapping. "Sorry about this, Kellie," he said out of the side of his mouth.

"It was inevitable," she whispered back.

The din died down. "Hi, everyone. I didn't expect a greeting like this when it's my sister's engagement party. We don't want to intrude on yours or Tom's happiness, Beth, so let me just explain a few things so you can all enjoy the rest of the party. I understand you're under the impression that Kellie and I are married. It's not true."

At that remark, expressions sobered. "We had to pretend to be married to smoke out the killer."

"Well, I'll be," one of his aunts exclaimed.

"It turned out there were two of them. Identical twin brothers who'd murdered three other women back east before they targeted Kellie."

Murmurs of horror came from the group. "Those two criminals have been arrested. Kellie is now free to continue traveling the rodeo circuit before she competes in the Finals in Las Vegas in December. Her next rodeo will be in South Dakota this coming weekend."

She tugged on his arm and whispered, "Do you mind if I say something?"

"Go ahead."

"We're together tonight because we're working on a statement to put out on my blog and the newspaper about the lie I told people. It was necessary to my case that the stalkers believe I had a husband. His captain and my parents agreed.

"Ranger Vance's brilliant idea frustrated those killers, who lost focus long enough for him and the other Texas Rangers to close in on them faster than anyone expected. But let me assure you he wouldn't have missed his sister's party for the world. Under the very real circumstances of life and death, I learned for a fact he loves his sister and family more than anything." A few *ohs* of sentiment followed her comment. "That's why I agreed to come with him. We'll finish up police business after the party. Since I'm the only girl in my family, too, I know how important this night is to Beth and her future husband. Please forget we're here now and go on with your celebration."

Cy already knew he was in love with Kellie, but her ability to think on her feet under difficult circumstances added to her stature in his eyes. She was a living miracle.

AFTER CY SAID he wanted to leave the party, his mother walked Kellie to the door. He and his father were behind them. "You've been through an experience I wouldn't wish on my worst enemy." Her son looked a lot like his attractive mother. She had those dark blue eyes, too.

"Cy was heroic in his treatment of me. If my choice of words sounds strange to you, let me assure you chivalry isn't dead. Because of how he handled everything, it took away a lot of the horror." Kellie felt her eyes smarting. "He made me believe in him, that he could do anything if I went along with his plan. He affected my parents the same way."

His mother's eyes misted over. "He always did have the quality that instills confidence. Cy's father wanted him to go into law, but he had another dream. A dangerous one. To think he saved your life makes me ashamed that I ever wished he'd find another career."

"Then you can imagine how grateful I am to him."

It was obvious Cy's mother had found a way to live with it, but Kellie was afraid she would never be able to get over her fear for his safety. She knew herself too well. To live in constant agony because of a man's occupation wasn't for her. A wave of deep sorrow washed over her, knowing that after tonight she wouldn't be seeing him again.

"Our family will be rooting for you in December."

"Thank you, Mrs. Vance."

"Call me Annette."

She smiled. "Your daughter is darling and Tom seems like a wonderful man. You must be so happy for her."

"I am. She's never given me grief. Cy has been a different story, but that's because he's definitely his own person."

"I found that out."

The older woman reached out to hug her. Then Cy's father gave her a hug.

"I understand you were the model of bravery during your ordeal. My son grew up esteeming that quality once he found out we had real Texas Ranger blood running in our veins."

"I've heard the story, and the more I learn about Cy and his colleagues, the more I know all the legends about the Rangers are true."

Cy reached her side. "What are you two talking about?"

"You and the Lone Ranger riding your trusty steed Rosco P.," she teased.

His dad laughed and winked at Kellie. "Drive home safe."

"We will. It was a lovely party."

She hurried ahead of Cy to reach his car. But he

overtook her and helped her into the passenger side. After they backed out of the driveway and headed toward Austin, he reached for her hand and wouldn't let go. "You were fabulous tonight."

"Your family is wonderful."

"Everyone thought *you* were wonderful." He squeezed her hand tighter before letting it go to make a turn.

"Beth looked the way every bride-to-be should look. Radiant with no cloud in her sky."

She felt his glance. "You said that with a degree of sadness." Cy was already picking up on her dark thoughts.

"I didn't realize it was that obvious." She changed the subject and they talked about the different relatives and friends she'd met at the party. They kept the tone light, but once they'd reached her town house and had gone inside, he shut the door and put his hands on her shoulders from behind.

"Tell me what was eating at you during the ride home," he murmured against the side of her neck.

This was going to be the hard part. She moved away, forcing him to drop his hands. "Before we talk, I want you to read the draft I've written for the blog. And after that I'd like your opinion on what we should give to the newspaper. The *Statesman* and the *Chronicle* have been asking for an article. My laptop is upstairs. I'll bring it down and we can work at the table."

She tossed her clutch on the couch and rushed away, praying he wouldn't try to stop her. When she'd told herself she could quit Cy cold turkey, that was before

she realized she was madly in love with him. This was
the kind of love that would never go away, not in a mil-
lennium.

CY REMOVED HIS suit jacket and tie. He hung them over
the back of one of the kitchen chairs before sitting down
in another one. This place had been like home to him
for a week. Now he was a guest.

While he waited for her, he pulled out his phone.
There were messages from the guys, but those could
wait. He listened to the one from the captain. "Call
me on my private line ASAP. I have some news on the
Ravelo case."

Since Kellie hadn't come down yet, he phoned his
boss. "TJ?"

"I'm glad you called, Cy. There was a homicide over
in East Austin tonight around ten. It turns out someone shot one of the hostages taken by Ravelo during
the robbery two years ago. His name is listed in the
file as Jorge Montoya. Go over to the morgue and see
what the autopsy revealed before you come into work
in the morning."

Kellie walked in the kitchen while they were talking
and put her laptop on the table. He stood up and turned
his back to her while he finished the conversation.

"I've been studying the case. Maybe Montoya was
in on the robbery with Ravelo. But when he didn't get
his cut of the take, he gunned for Ravelo and got liqui-
dated by a hit man or Ravelo himself. I'll find out when
I'm down in Brownsville."

"Trust you to come up with a better possibility than anything the police have been able to figure out."

"It's a guess."

"Nine times out of ten your guesses beat the hell out of everyone else's."

"Don't I wish. Good night, TJ."

When he hung up and turned around, Kellie had taken a seat at the table. "I'm sorry if I intruded on a private conversation."

He bristled. "You could never intrude. The captain and I were going over a new case."

"So I gathered." She averted her eyes and opened her laptop. "Take a look at what I wrote the other night. Tell me what needs to be added or deleted." She was all business.

Cy moved it around so he could read it. The sooner they got this out of the way, the sooner he could find out what was causing her to pull away from him. At the park before the party, she hadn't hidden anything from him. The old saying that he thought he'd died and gone to heaven had summed it up best. After that, how could she change so fast from the warm, loving woman he was crazy about to someone he didn't recognize?

To all my fans—If you haven't watched the news, then you may not know that I've been the target of two stalker brothers who have made my life a living hell for the past month. The Texas Rangers were called in to help me.

In order to draw these criminals out, I had to pretend to be married in order to trap them. Now that they've been arrested in a cunning sting, I can announce that my marriage was a brilliant piece of fiction that kept me alive until they were caught. Besides my wonderful parents, I owe the Texas Rangers my life.

But I'll have you know that the husband I made up truly is the man of my dreams. Maybe one day... In the meantime, I'll be working hard riding the circuit until December, when I'll be participating in the National Finals Rodeo in Las Vegas. See you there! Long live the rodeo!

He sucked in his breath. "I can find no fault with it."

"Good. I thought I could send the first two paragraphs to the newspapers. But I'll put the entire article on my blog."

"Again I think what you've written is just right. One question, though." He shot her a glance. "Why did you use the word *cunning*?"

"Because you had to fight fire with fire. It's what you do. No one else comes close to your genius. *Cunning* means deceitful, crafty and full of guile. Those words describe the two stalkers who would have murdered me if it hadn't been for you. That's why you're such a brilliant Ranger."

He rubbed the side of his jaw, trying to figure her out. "Why are you suddenly distancing yourself from me?"

She sat back in the chair and stared at him through veiled eyes. "Because you became my hero throughout this reign of terror. My prince, if you like. But when you brought it to an end, I realized you do this every day for a living. You move on from one ghastly, gory case to another, and then another and another. On the phone just now I heard you discussing a hit man and a robbery.

"Those aren't just words to me anymore. A hit man is someone who actually goes out and kills people. Those brothers were planning to kill me. They became real. The whole situation became agonizingly frightening when Dan started stalking me. Then he tried to kill *you*. I've lived through a nightmare and will never be the same again."

"Kellie—"

"Let me finish. The other day Dad brought up the possibility of my getting therapy. I didn't want to hear it, but I think he's right. Forgive me for throwing myself at you in the car. I didn't know any other way to express my feelings. It shows how off-kilter I am. You're a man and you responded like any red-blooded man. But I'm a wreck, Cy."

His stomach roiled. "So what are you saying? That you take it all back? That you don't want to see me again?"

"Yes— No— I'm not explaining myself right. I would love to be with you again and again, but I can't bring myself to do it because—"

"Because what?"

"I'm afraid I'll lose you while you're in the line of duty. The other night you made yourself a target for Dan to shoot you. I was there, and I was dying inside. I went through that experience with you. Don't you see?" She got to her feet.

"I know that when you go to work, you're going to

put yourself in jeopardy laying your life on the line every day, or night, depending on the circumstances." She clung to the back of her chair. "You asked me why I sounded sad tonight. I'll tell you why.

"I saw your sister and her fiancé so happy, and I was so envious. She never has to worry when he goes to work at your dad's law firm that he'll be shot or blown to bits by a bomb or stabbed to death. I know there aren't any guarantees in this life for any of us, but he'll probably live a long full life and raise a family with her.

"I don't see that in your stars, Cy. I'm being honest. I couldn't handle it if anything happened to you. Though I'll never forget you, if I don't see you again, hopefully in time I'll fall in love and get married to someone who's—"

"Safe?" He cut her off.

"Yes!"

"Where's the barrel racer who stares down danger every time she enters the arena?"

"For heaven's sake, Cy. You can't compare that to what you do. I don't care about me. It's you who matters! Just hearing about this new case you're going to work on makes me sick to my stomach. I don't want to think about it. I know someone has to protect us from the evil out there, but I don't want the man I love to be the one who does it."

He grabbed hold of the table, hoping he'd heard her right. "You *love* me?"

She swallowed hard. "What do you think I've been saying all this time? Yes, I love you. I'm madly in love

with you. Isn't that crazy? We only met nine days ago, yet I know to the marrow of my bones it's true.

"But I don't want to be in love with you. Your poor parents didn't have a choice when you made up your mind what career to go into, but I *do*. So I'm going to ride away from you while I still can."

"That's not going to solve anything," he said in a grating voice.

"Maybe not, but when I'm off on my rodeo circuit, I'll be spared knowing that you were shot and killed by some lawless felon while I was gone. I don't want to be anywhere around when that happens. Now, I think you'd better go. The vet is going to be out early in the morning to give my horses a checkup."

The fact that she loved him would help him get through all the other things she'd said that he hadn't wanted to hear. She needed more time.

"Will you let me hold you for a little while before I leave?"

She shook her head. "No. I don't dare. Kissing you in the car was a big mistake."

Like hell it was…

"Kellie? Look at me."

"Please don't ask me. I enjoyed the evening with your family. Let's let it rest there with that memory."

"Would it help if I told you I'm head over heels in love with you?"

"For the second time, you mean?" she asked in a sharp tone. "If I recall, you told me you barely escaped marriage the first time around."

"That's because I wasn't ready for a commitment."

"Even so, someone will come into your future who will be the right fit for you. Maybe a woman in law enforcement who can deal with the risks to her own life and yours. They say the third time's the charm."

"You're being intentionally cruel, but it's not working. You and I were on a collision course from the moment we bumped into each other in Bandera."

"That's what they said about the last meteor coming toward Earth. But before it got caught into our gravity, its orbital path suddenly missed us and flew in another direction."

"Your metaphor doesn't apply to us. We got caught in the gravity you and I created together. There's no greater force. You can take off for South Dakota, but we'll never be able to escape each other's pull."

"I pray you're wrong," she said with tears in her voice. "Goodbye, Cy. As I heard Vic say to you, watch your back. Might I add, keep Sylvia close. She gets to go with you wherever you go because she has no issues. She even gets to sleep under your pillow and will be with you to the end. What a lucky woman."

Kellie... Kellie...

He reached for his jacket and tie. "Will you walk me to the door?"

"I'd rather not." She clung to the chair back. "Is this new case going to take you to Brownsville?"

"Maybe, but it's nothing for you to be concerned about."

"You see what I mean? Already I'm sick with worry because there are so many killings down there and you haven't even left my house."

"I'm sorry you heard me on the phone."

"So am I. Forgive me for being so awful to you, Cy. I wouldn't be alive today if you hadn't come to my rescue. Please go before I make everything worse."

She was in so much turmoil, he realized there was nothing he could do right now. "I'm leaving." He crossed through the living room to the door. After opening it, he waited to see if she would call him back, but it didn't happen. The evening had turned into a nightmare of new proportions.

Cy pushed in the night lock and shut the door. After reaching the car, he sat there behind the wheel for a few minutes. Kellie loved him. But after what she'd lived through, if he asked her to marry him, then he needed to get into a different line of work.

The thought of leaving the Rangers tore him up inside.

The thought of losing Kellie ripped his heart out.

Chapter Ten

"This is Lydia Olson from Rider Rodeo Connection in Rapid City, South Dakota, for the Black Hills Pro Rodeo. The reigning champion barrel racer for tonight's win is Kellie Parrish with a 13.90 score. You're just racking up the wins, girl. Congratulations!"

"Thank you so much."

"I had to pull out my cheat sheet to list all your stats. You're a Wrangler NFR Qualifier ten times, a College National Finals Qualifier two times, the National High School Rodeo Finals Qualifier four times, and the Pro Wrangler Finals winner in Oklahoma City, Oklahoma, three times. And this year has been the best for you so far."

Kellie nodded. "It's been a good year for me." A year that had changed her life in ways she would never have imagined, but she didn't want to think about Cy right now. "My horses have been terrific and I'm hoping to do well at Finals in December. There's a lot of money to be won and the competition is tough. You're only as good as your last win, so you can't let down. I've got six more rodeos to go before I head to Las Vegas."

"You've thrilled the folks tonight and I wouldn't be surprised if you come out number one in Las Vegas."

"I'm excited to try."

"Where are you headed next?"

"Cheyenne, Wyoming."

"Well, we wish you luck. Thank you for talking to us for a few minutes. What plans do you have to celebrate tonight?"

"I'm going to go pet my horse before I do anything else. She was perfect tonight."

"There it is, folks! Kellie Parrish, who stunned the crowd on her champion horse, Trixie."

"Thank you."

Kellie left the arena and hurried to the rear of the pavilion to see Trixie. Cody had already taken care of Starburst.

Trixie neighed when she saw Kellie, who rushed up to her and threw an arm around her neck. "You were wonderful, Trixie. Here." She pulled a horsey treat out of her jeans pocket. The palomino gobbled it noisily. Kellie chuckled as she led her by a lead rope out the back of the facility to the trailer.

For the next half hour she went through her routine of removing the saddle and bridle, followed by a brushdown before loading her inside the trailer for the night. Earlier in the day Kellie had mucked out her stall, where she'd provided water and had put fresh hay in the net.

"Good night, Trixie. Dream of grassy meadows and sunshine."

Her horse neighed in response before Kellie shut the door.

"That horse is half human."

"Hey, Cody." Her dark-haired buddy had parked next to her. "How's Starburst?"

"I rode her for a while. She's in good shape. Great job out there tonight. I've never seen you ride better. Frankly, after knowing what you've just been through, I don't see how you stayed so focused."

The determination to erase Cy from her mind had played a big factor.

She smiled at Cody. "I couldn't do any of it without you, but I guess you know that. We've made some good money. Depending on what happens at Finals, we should both have enough to get started on our careers after the New Year."

"That's what Jenny and I are counting on. Want to celebrate with us tonight? We're going to grab a bite and take in a movie."

"Thanks, but I'm exhausted. I'll follow you back to the RV campground and call it a night."

They both started up their trucks and drove the short distance to the outskirts of Rapid City. After checking on her horse once more, she visited Starburst and gave her some horsey treats. Then she went into her trailer and took a shower. Once ready for bed, she phoned her parents. They celebrated her win by informing her they would fly to Greeley, Colorado, in two weeks to watch her performance. What would she do without her loving, supportive parents?

After she got off the phone, she posted a message on her blog to keep her fans informed of tonight's performance. Once that was accomplished, she returned phone calls from Olivia and Sally, who told her Manny was competing at the rodeo in Greeley. Kellie would look forward to seeing them there and introducing Sally's bull-rider-champion husband to her folks.

At last ready for bed, she got under the covers and turned on the radio. But the country-and-western station played the kind of music that talked of breakups and unhappiness. She turned to KBHB broadcasting from Sturgis, South Dakota. Lots of farm news and world news interspersed, but she wasn't able to concentrate and finally shut it off.

In the dark of the night she couldn't kid herself. She'd been hoping she'd hear from Cy all week. It hadn't happened. Kellie hadn't seen him since last Sunday night. They'd parted on such an ugly note, it had left her shaken. Was he deep into his new case?

When she couldn't stand it any longer, she looked up Luckey's number on her contacts list. The temptation to find out what he knew about Cy had been driving her crazy. Tonight she gave in to it and phoned him. The call went directly to his voice mail, but she held off from leaving a message and hung up. She was a fool. Luckey would know she'd called and would probably tell Cy. So much for going cold turkey. She eventually fell asleep, furious at herself for succumbing to the impulse.

The next morning Kellie got up and dressed. After eating a bowl of cereal, she planned to walk both her horses before they all started the drive to Wyoming. On her way out of the trailer, her cell rang. She checked the caller ID and felt a swift surge of adrenaline. It was Luckey. She answered on the third ring.

"Hi, Luckey."

"Hi, yourself. I saw you called last night, but I didn't get a chance to return it until now."

"I shouldn't have bothered you."

"Surely you didn't think I'd mind."

Like Cy, he had those special qualities and charm that made him stand out. "No. I'll be honest. Ranger Vance and I said goodbye last Sunday night. Since then I've been out on the circuit. But I couldn't help overhearing part of a conversation he had with the captain. It had something to do with a case that could take him to Brownsville." She moistened her lips nervously. "I've been a little worried because of all the tension on the border."

"I'm on another assignment and can't discuss any cases, but as far as I know all is well with him."

"I guess I'm having a hard time letting this go. After he saved my life, naturally I don't want to see him injured or worse."

"It's understandable considering he went undercover to protect you. You wouldn't be human if you didn't come out of your experience unchanged. I'll tell you a secret. When I applied to join the Rangers, there was a saying printed at the top. 'Decide that you want it more than you are afraid of it.' I thought about it long and hard before I submitted it."

Kellie had to stifle a moan. "That explains the spirit of the Sons of the Forty."

"It explains why you're a rodeo star," he replied. "Not everyone is driven by the same passion. Since the guys and I saw you at the Bandera Rodeo, we're all planning on you winning the World Championship."

"Thank you for those kind words. For everything," she half whispered. "You've given me a lot to think about. Watch your back, Ranger." She hung up to prevent further conversation.

Decide that you want it more than you are afraid of it. Such a simple statement, yet such profound wisdom.

AFTER HIS FLIGHT from Brownsville to Austin on Saturday evening, Cy went straight to his house to get some much-needed sleep. So far the Ravelo case wasn't opening up for him. If there were any family members still living there, Cy hadn't found evidence of one. He'd been concentrating in the wrong place and would pursue his angle on Montoya's tie-in to the robbery now that he was back.

Sunday morning he got up late and checked his laptop for emails. Nothing from Kellie, no phone calls. She had his cell-phone number, but it seemed she'd meant what she'd said two weeks ago. She didn't want to love him. *Damn* if she wasn't proving it by her silence.

He glanced at her rodeo schedule on the website, then read her latest entry on her blog. Last night she'd had another winning performance in Cheyenne, Wyoming. Two wins in two weeks. Without the specter of the stalkers, she was going ahead full steam on her road to a dazzling championship in Las Vegas.

In a dark mood and feeling empty, he left for the office. On Sundays it was fairly quiet around there and he'd be able to get through the paperwork that had been piling up while he'd been gone. Halfway through it, his cell rang. The caller ID said Bronco Parrish.

His heartbeat quickened and he clicked on immediately. "Mr. Parrish?"

"No. It's Nadine Parrish."

"Hello, Nadine. How are you?"

"I've been fine until just now."

"What's wrong?"

"I'm sorry to bother you, Ranger Vance. Maybe it's nothing, but I found something in Kellie's mailbox. I went over to her town house this morning to check on things and water her plants. Maybe this isn't important, but I thought you should know."

He frowned. "What is it?"

"Besides her usual mail, there was another typewritten envelope with her address, but no return address. It's postmarked two days ago. I brought the mail inside, but I haven't opened it."

"Are you still at her condo?"

"Yes."

"Don't touch it. I'll be right over and park in front."

Cy's mind raced with possibilities as he left headquarters and drove to Kellie's town house. Maybe it was simply a note from a friend, but something in his gut told him that wasn't the case. He reached into the glove compartment and pulled out a pair of latex gloves from a box he kept there.

Nadine had opened the front door and was waiting for him. Judging by the lines on her face, she was worried. They'd all assumed this case was over. He hoped to heaven he was wrong about a third party being involved with the stalkers.

She gave him a hug he reciprocated. By tacit agreement they went into the kitchen and sat down at the table, where she'd left the mail. The white envelope stood out from the rest of the bills and ads.

"Let's see what's in here." He put on the gloves and opened it.

You're a little *fresa* who should have been eliminated a long time ago. No one wants a badass like you around in your skinny designer jeans.

This wasn't the language that came from either stalker. The type was different. If he didn't miss his guess, it was sent by a jealous female. Dan could have been using her, possibly her car. He lifted the typewritten note to his nose. There was a faint smell. Not perfume. Because it had been posted only two days ago, maybe residue lotion had clung to the paper. Kellie's mom eyed him nervously.

"What do you think?"

He didn't show her what was typed. "I'm not sure, but you were wise to call me. I'll take this to headquarters. If you're through here, I'd rather you didn't come back until I've done an investigation. I'll let you know when I deem it safe. Whatever you do, don't tell Kellie. I understand she's come in first at both rodeos so far. Let's not throw her off track unless we have to. If I think she needs to know, I'll get in contact with her."

"I agree. Thank you so much for coming right over."

After Nadine locked the front door, he walked her to her car then got into his own. On the way to the office, he phoned Vic, who'd put on his voice mail. Cy left him a message and asked if he'd meet him at headquarters if at all possible.

The second he got in his office, he opened the paper file on Kellie and searched through the evidence, but he didn't see the report on the Sentra sedan. While he was studying the notepaper already in the file, Vic walked in.

"Hey, Vic—I'm sorry to bother you on a family day."

"It's all right. Jeremy is at his aunt's house playing with his cousin Randy right now. For you to be here on Sunday meant your message was urgent. Have you gotten a break on the Ravelo case?"

"No. That's why I'm back in Austin, but something else has come up and I'm afraid it could be serious. Here's a pair of gloves." Cy pulled them out of the box in his bottom drawer. "Take a look at this. Kellie's mother found it with the mail when she went over to her town house this morning."

Vic put the gloves on and checked the note, then looked at the envelope. "This was mailed two days ago from the Del Valle post office."

"That's only seven miles southeast of here. Where's the paperwork on the Sentra sedan impounded the night of the takedown?"

"Maybe forensics didn't send it up yet, but it should be on the computer. What are you thinking?"

"I'm wondering if Dan had a girlfriend who lives around there and was using her car."

"I took a look at it. A 1999 model that looked like it's been through a war."

"Maybe she found out about Kellie and couldn't stand the competition. This note has a scent. The other notes don't. They're not made of the same kind of paper and the language isn't like Dan's."

His friend picked it up to test. "You're right, but news of the arrests has been all over the internet and TV. If such a person exists, why would she send Kellie a note now?"

"I don't know, Vic. It's just a hunch, nothing more, but I don't like it. I want to find the person who mailed this. For a start I need the name of the owner of that car."

"I'll phone Stan at home. Maybe he can tell us where the report is backed up in the system. I have his home phone number on a list in my office." He pulled off the gloves and tossed them into the wastebasket. "Give me a second and I'll get it."

Vic had been gone only a minute when he came right back and handed Cy a file. "The report was on my desk. I guess they thought you'd be in Brownsville longer, so they gave it to me. It must have been put there after I went home yesterday."

He sat down next to Cy and they pored over it. "The present owner is Martina Martinez with an address in Garfield, Texas. That explains the postmark when they moved the Garfield post office to Del Valle."

"She has a rap sheet for petty crimes starting at the age of fifteen. At the present age of twenty-one, her last known address is 16 Spring Street, and her last known employment is a manicurist job at the Travis County Hair Salon."

"Maybe he hit on her when he went in to get a manicure or another wig or some such thing."

"That's what I'm thinking," Cy murmured. "Her car went missing the night we arrested Dan. I think we both know why she didn't call the police to report it stolen."

"No doubt she stole it off someone else."

"Let's find out right now. I'll drive us."

They left the building and took off. The GPS guided them to a small bungalow in a run-down neighborhood on Spring Street in Garfield. Cy parked two houses away from the actual address and turned off the engine.

"While you knock on the front door, I'll move around the back so any escape is covered."

"Right."

They'd worked together for a long time and could read each other's minds. Cy walked to the rear and planted himself next to the back door. It didn't take long before it opened and the woman they'd hoped to find came flying out as he suspected she would. Cy caught her tattooed arm and forced her hands behind her back to cuff her. She let go with a stream of Spanish curse words, trying to kick him. By this time Vic had joined him. "I've called for backup."

"Good. Martina Martinez, you're under arrest for evading police during an official investigation. You have the right to remain silent until an attorney is present. If you don't have one, the court will appoint one for you."

An older Hispanic woman of maybe fifty hid herself

behind the partially opened door. "What do you want with my Martina? She's done nothing wrong."

Vic's hands were on his hips. "She shouldn't have run when I asked if I could talk to her."

"What do you want with me?" the suspect cried. "I haven't done nothing."

"Where's the blue Sentra car belonging to you?" Cy questioned.

"I don't know what you're talking about."

"Your rap sheet says you're the owner, but it showed up at a town house in Austin. The man driving it has been arrested for murder. The police already have your fingerprints on file from your former arrests. When they match them to the ones found in the car along with his prints, then you'll be going to prison along with the guy for being an accomplice."

"There's no guy!"

"Sure there is. Is he your boyfriend? How about that threatening letter you mailed to Kellie Parrish from the Del Valle post office?"

She tried to spit at him. "You can't prove I sent anything to that spoiled *fresa*."

Convicted by her own mouth. *Fresa* meant "strawberry," a derogatory term she'd written in her note.

"Your fingerprints will be all over that letter when it's examined. What happened? Did he take off in your car to see Kellie and didn't come back? Did that make you so angry you lashed out at her?" Cy heard sirens getting closer by the second.

"Shut your mouth, *chota*!"

Cy had hit a nerve. Nothing could have pleased him

more than to be called a crooked cop. "We'll let you tell that to the judge."

Vic took her other side. They dragged her around to the front of the house while the older woman screamed at them. Neighbors in the area came out of their houses to see what was going on. Two police cars had converged on the scene. The officers took over and put her in the back of one of the patrol cars. After giving information for the incident report, Cy walked back to the car with Vic.

"I'll ask TJ to get a warrant so the crew can search the house for signs that Dan might have stayed there from time to time. Someone needs to take down a statement from the mother."

When they got back to headquarters, Vic left to go pick up his son. He invited Cy to come over to his house later and they'd kick back with a beer. That sounded good since Cy dreaded going home to his empty house.

He went into his office to leave a message on the captain's phone about the arrest of the Martinez woman. Then he phoned Nadine Parrish to give her the news. She wasn't the only one greatly relieved. For a second when he'd first seen that letter postmarked only two days ago, his heart sank at imagining there was still another stalker out there.

The two of them decided Kellie didn't need to know anything about this until her tour of the circuit was over. Before they hung up, Nadine informed him she and her husband were flying to Greeley the next Saturday to watch her compete in the rodeo.

Kellie's mother could have no conception of the kind

of pain he'd been in for the past two weeks. All he could say was he hoped she'd make the best time and he wished her well.

"I'll tell her."

With that phone call over, he was emotionally drained and left for his car. Before he turned on the engine, he received a call from Luckey and clicked on.

"I'm glad to catch you, Cy. Are you still in Brownsville?"

"Nope. I came home when my lead there went dry. It's a good thing I did." For the next few minutes he told his friend about the letter and the arrest of the Martinez woman.

"That must have knocked you for a loop when you saw another note."

"I have to admit it did."

"Does Kellie know about it?"

"Not yet. Her mother will probably tell her when she and her husband meet up with her in Greeley to watch her performance."

"Why not you?"

"Because we parted company two weeks ago."

"As in…"

"I won't be seeing her again."

"Cy… there's something you ought to know."

He inhaled sharply. "What's that?"

"She phoned me last weekend."

"Kellie *what*?"

"Yeah. I was on a case and couldn't answer it. She didn't leave a message. The next morning when I saw that she had called, I phoned her to find out what she wanted. At first she was apologetic for bothering me. Then she asked if you were down in Brownsville.

"I told her I couldn't discuss a case, but assured her all was well with you. She thanked me and then just before hanging up she said, 'I guess I'm having a hard time letting this go. After he saved my life, naturally I don't want to see him injured or worse.'"

Cy bowed his head. In one week she'd broken down to Luckey. To Cy's joy, the ice was cracking. He'd warned her they could never escape each other's pull. After hearing this bit of telling news, the longing for her was so great he knew he had to do something about it. Knowing her folks were flying to Colorado next week gave him an idea, but he'd have to clear it with his boss.

"Thanks for being my friend, Luckey. I owe you."

Chapter Eleven

14.00. Second place for the night at the Oklahoma rodeo. Not good enough.

Cynthia Lyman had taken first with a 13.95.

"It wasn't your fault, Starburst." Kellie threw an arm around her neck and fed her a treat. She'd been losing concentration and there was only one reason why. Instead of getting over Cy, her love for him was stronger than ever. She was dying to talk to him, to be held and kissed. But she needed to nail some first places at the three upcoming rodeos in Texas in order to maintain the highest average. That wouldn't happen if she didn't snap out of it.

The most despondent she'd been since leaving Austin, she walked Starburst back to the trailer and loaded her inside. Once she'd taken care of her, she drove to the RV campground where she and Cody were staying.

There were headlights behind her she could see through the side-view mirror on her truck. Someone else was coming into the RV park. She wound her way through to their reserved area. The lights stayed with her. Maybe it was Cody.

Soon she turned into their spot and could see Cody's truck and trailer ahead in the distance. Her cell rang. She knew it was Cody. He always phoned her when he saw she was back. After stopping the truck, she clicked on without looking at the caller ID.

"I know...you don't have to say anything, Cody. I didn't have a good night."

"14.00 nabbed you a second place. From where I was sitting, you wowed the audience."

At the sound of the familiar male voice, she almost went into cardiac arrest. *"Cy?"* Kellie was trying to comprehend it. "You were in the audience tonight?"

"Yup. I flew into Oklahoma City and rented a car at the airport so I could drive to the arena and watch your performance. I wanted to join you while you were walking Starburst to the trailer, but I didn't want to frighten you. I've probably made things worse by following you. Thus the phone call."

Kellie was speechless.

He'd come all this way to see her.

She forgot everything and scrambled out of the truck. He was moving toward her. She couldn't get to him fast enough and started running. He caught her up in his arms and swung her around like a bride.

"Cy—" But anything else she would have said was stifled by the hunger of his kiss. Delirious with love and wanting, she kissed him back without thinking about anything else. All she could do was show him what he meant to her. They melted together, trying to become one.

"I love you, Cy. You were right about everything. I miss you too horribly to let you go."

"That's all I need to hear. I'm in the middle of a big case and have to be back at the airport in a half hour to catch the red-eye from New York to Austin. It makes one stop here. We don't have much time. Come and get in the car with me. We have to talk fast."

She wanted to scream that it wasn't fair to experience this much rapture, only to have it snatched away in so short a time. But this was Cy's life. Even working a dangerous case, he'd come for her. She had to find a way to deal with it, because he really was her whole world.

After they got into the car, he pulled her to him. She needed his kiss as she needed air to breathe. What they were doing was devouring each other, but there wasn't enough time to pack in all their feelings in a matter of minutes.

"I love *you*, Kellie. You're so much a part of me at this point, I can't live without you."

"I can't either, darling. I've been so afraid of loving you for fear I'd lose you. But Luckey told me something that straightened out my dilemma in a hurry."

"He said you called him."

"Obviously I couldn't bear even a week apart from you. He told me about what was written on the application when he wanted to become a Texas Ranger. It said, 'Decide you want it more than you're afraid of it.'" She looked into those dark blue eyes. "I want you more… so much more you can't even imagine."

"Good old Luckey," he whispered against her lips before driving his kiss deeper. After he lifted his head, he reached into his Western shirt pocket. "Will you marry me for real this time?" He held up a diamond ring.

She let out a cry. "It's the same one you gave me before. I thought it was property from the agency's warehouse."

The smile she loved broke out on his face. "It's not the same one, exactly. But it's the same style, yes. I wanted the ring to look like the one you wore when we pretended to be man and wife. I think I wanted our marriage to be real from the beginning." He slid it home on her ring finger.

Tears filled her eyes to feel it back where it belonged. "So did I. The blog piece I put on about our fake marriage wasn't fake to me. I meant every one of those words you said were over-the-top."

He pressed his cheek to hers. "I said them because I wanted to think you meant them, but I was afraid that dream could never become a reality." He found her mouth and kissed her passionately, over and over again. "Have you put your disclaimer in the paper and on your blog site yet? I've been too busy to look."

"No. I've been holding off. It's because I haven't been able to take back the words I wrote. I'm afraid they're written in my heart forever. I could feel myself falling for you after your captain first brought me into your office at the agency. There you were again, the Ranger I'd bumped into in Bandera. You were the most glorious sight this cowgirl had ever seen, standing there in the sun in your Stetson."

"Someday I'll tell you all the things I thought about you that day, but we don't have much more time. How would you feel about getting married secretly in Fort Worth three weeks from now? I'll arrange to take the weekend off."

"Only the weekend?"

"I can't take more while I'm still on this case. We could be married by a justice of the peace in the afternoon, then I'll watch you win your last rodeo. We'll honeymoon for a day on our way back to Austin. After Finals we'll have a family wedding at the church and a reception."

She burrowed her face in his neck. "I think it's perfect, but I don't know how I'm going to last until Forth Worth without you."

"I'll phone you every opportunity I get."

"If you're undercover, I don't want to know about it."

"That's good. We'll both be happier that way. Tomorrow I'll tell my folks we're engaged."

"I'll do the same and inform the parents we want to be married right after Finals. I'll tell Mom to call your mom. The two of them will get together to plan the wedding."

"My folks have been waiting for this day forever. I have a three-week vacation coming up whenever I want to take it. The last night of Finals will be Saturday, December 12. We could get married on New Year's Day and take off for that long honeymoon you announced on your blog."

She crushed him to her. "I can't believe this is really happening."

"You will." After another kiss, "I have to leave for

the airport now, sweetheart. Come on. I'll walk you to your trailer."

"You don't need to do that. I know you're in a hurry." On a groan, she gave him one more kiss to last until they saw each other again in Fort Worth. "Never forget how much I love you, Ranger Vance."

Somehow she forced herself to get out of his car. She ran to the trailer and opened the back to check on Starburst. The headlights of his rental car shone on her and her horse. When she couldn't see them any longer, she turned to Starburst and half sobbed for joy against her neck.

"He loves me, Starburst. See my engagement ring?"

Her horse nickered in response as if to say she already knew.

KELLIE HAD A hard time keeping her secret from Cody, even though he knew she was engaged for real. On Friday they reached Fort Worth. After getting settled at the RV campground, she told him she had some shopping to do in town and would work out with the horses later in the day.

After several stores she found a lovely oyster-colored two-piece lined wedding suit with long sleeves and pearl buttons. The jacket had lace trim on the collar and around the hem. She wanted to look bridal yet smart and sophisticated for this fabulous man she was marrying. This outfit was for him alone. She bought matching high heels and a beaded clutch bag. A new pair of pearl earrings caught her eye plus new underwear and a nightgown, the kind she'd never worn in her life. All soft lace and tiny straps.

Once she was back in Austin, she'd hunt for a gorgeous wedding dress with her mom. Her parents were thrilled Cy had proposed and were already planning a New Year's Day wedding with his parents.

Excited out of her mind because she was marrying Cy in the morning, she hurried back to the RV park and exercised both her horses. She told Cody she'd be going into town in the morning, but would be back by noon to prepare the horses for the drive to the arena.

That evening she put her children to bed and she got started working on herself. First to wash her hair, then do her nails and toenails.

Cy would fly into Forth Worth in the morning. Everyone would presume he was out of town on a case. They planned to meet in the lobby of the Fort Worth Police Administration Building on West Belnap at 9:30 a.m. He'd arranged everything and Justice of the Peace Wilford Hayes would marry them.

Trust her fiancé to want their marriage to take place at the police bureau. As for Kellie, she didn't care where it happened, as long as it did!

At a quarter to nine the next morning of November 7, she left for the police administration building, not wanting to be late. The parking was in a lot adjacent to the building. She drove in and parked her truck. As she walked out and across the street, she received so many wolf whistles and horn honks, it was embarrassing.

"That's some lucky dude!" a guy called out from his cement truck.

She was almost to the doors of the building when she caught sight of the most handsome man she'd ever seen. He stood in front of the doors holding a small florist box. He was wearing a light gray suit and dazzling white shirt. *Cy.*

"I'm the lucky dude all right."

Those piercing dark blue eyes were alive with desire as they swept over her. "Good heavens you're gorgeous." He pulled her into his arms and kissed her right on the street where everyone could see them. "These are for you. Let me pin them on."

While she stood there in a daze, he undid the lid and fastened a gardenia corsage on her shoulder. People waited to go in until he'd finished and had opened the door for her. He ushered her inside and kept his arm around her waist all the way to the elevator. "If it was your plan to take my breath, you've succeeded."

"I'm out of breath myself. I didn't know three weeks without seeing you could be so long. It's embarrassing how much I love you."

They got out on the next floor and walked down the hall to Judge Hayes's office. The secretary smiled and told them to be seated while she let the judge know they had arrived. Cy put the corsage box on the next seat over and clasped her hand in his.

"If you only knew how long I've been waiting for this moment." The throb in his deep voice resonated throughout her trembling body.

"I *do* know," she whispered back. Kellie would have said more, but the judge came into the outer office. The older man studied them for a moment.

"I believe I'm about to marry two of our state's most famous celebrities this morning. Come into my chambers." In an aside, he asked his secretary to find the other witness and join them. Cy squeezed Kellie's hand a little harder before walking her into the judge's office. He put the necessary papers on the desk. Two women came into the room after them and shut the door.

After the judge made the introductions, he asked Kellie and Cy to stand in front of him and join hands. They reached for each other automatically.

"It's my privilege to marry a fine Texas Ranger and our state's champion barrel racer. If you're ready, we'll begin the ceremony."

"We've been ready for a long time." Cy spoke boldly.

A smile broke out in the judge's eyes. "Is that true?" he asked Kellie.

"Yes."

"I can tell your husband-to-be is impatient."

"Not as impatient as I am, Your Honor."

"All right, then. Let's get to it. Kellie Parrish, do you promise to love him and cherish him and all that other stuff?"

Kellie couldn't help but laugh. "I do."

"Cyril Vance, do you promise to love her and cherish her and all that other stuff?"

Cy looked at her. "I do."

"We both do," Kellie said emotionally. "Forever."

The judge nodded. "Forever it is. I now pronounce you man and wife. Have you got a ring?"

Kellie stared at Cy in concern. He pulled the gold

band out of his pocket and handed it to her. She pushed it onto the ring finger of his left hand.

"Now you may kiss your bride, but make it a short one."

"I'm afraid I can't do that," her new husband said.

"I get your point. Well, don't just stand there—and don't forget you've got a rodeo tonight, Mrs. Vance. After the favor I've granted this superhero here in cutting this ceremony short, I expect a star performance."

"I'll try."

"I do believe you've got him hog-tied, and that's a real feat. According to his captain, who happens to be a good friend of mine, no female has been able to succeed until now. But I can see why she's brought you to your knees, Ranger Vance. If I were forty years younger, you'd have some tough competition. Now, get out of here and live a happy life!"

"Thank you, Judge," she said to him as Cy rushed her into the other room. No bride had ever had such a unique wedding ceremony.

Before she could take a breath, he drew her into his arms and gave her a kiss to die for. "Let's get back to your trailer. I'll drive. If an officer pulls us over, I'll flash my star."

This was a side of Cy she hadn't seen before. He was like a different person. Funny, playful. Life with him was going to be filled with surprises. She almost had to run to keep up with him. They flew down the hall. He didn't want to wait for the elevator. Instead he opted for the stairwell. Before she knew it, they were outside and headed across the street to the parking lot.

"The truck's down there on the right."

"I know where it is. I watched you drive in and park."

That was her Texas Ranger. Always ten steps ahead of everyone else, and he was her *husband*!

"The keys."

She rummaged in her beaded bag and handed them to him. After he helped her into the passenger side, he ran a hand over her thigh and leg before shutting the door. His touch, so unexpected and convulsive, had set her on fire.

On their way out he paid the fee and they took off for the RV park with her directing him. "How soon do we need to leave for the arena?"

She checked her watch. "An hour."

"No matter how high I go over the speed limit, that won't leave us time for a wedding night until after your win tonight."

What?

He shot her a glance. "You couldn't be as disappointed as I am, but I need a whole night to make love to my wife for the first time. Since I'm counting on you clocking the lowest time in your event, I'm going to have to be patient a little longer. While you get ready, I'll hitch the trailer to the truck and do any odd jobs you need doing."

Kellie loved him so terribly, her heart hurt.

Cy spoke the truth. Their wedding night wouldn't be perfect if she couldn't hold him all night long. But they'd wanted to be married today. Even though a price had to be paid, nothing in life had made her this happy.

When they drove up to her trailer, Cody was outside

it checking one of the tires. When he turned and saw the two of them in their wedding finery, a huge smile broke out on his face.

"Well, what do you know? You got hitched and beat me and my fiancée to the punch." He walked over to give her a hug and shake Cy's hand.

Cy wrapped his arm around Kellie. "We didn't want to wait any longer. Would you mind taking a couple of pictures of us with my cell phone? We need to record this day for posterity. One day we hope to have children who will deserve to see the way their gorgeous mother looked the day we got married."

"And their father," she added with tears in her eyes. They hadn't talked about children. There were still so many things they didn't know about each other. Every revelation made her love him more.

He fixed the phone so all Cody had to do was keep pressing the button.

Trust Cody, who behaved like a photographer at a photo shoot. He had them pose this way and that, and of course lined up a few shots of them kissing.

"Yeah, yeah. That's what we want," Cody teased them until she was red in the face.

"No one knows we got married except you, Cody," she informed him. "Where's Jenny?"

"Out shopping. I'll pick her up on the way to the arena."

"You can tell her, of course. Cy and I will be having a big church wedding after Finals. This wedding was just for us."

"You two have been through hell. I'm happy for you."

He handed Cy the phone. "I'm just going to put a little more air in this tire."

Cy reached for her hand and they walked to her trailer. "It's the painted blue key," she said as he looked at the key chain. He unlocked the door and they went inside. For a few minutes the world was shut out.

She heard the sigh that came out of him. He turned to her and removed the gardenias from her jacket. "I wouldn't want to smash these." He put them on a chair, then took off his suit jacket and tie. "How long will it take you to change into your riding clothes?" He'd started undoing the top buttons of his shirt.

"Five minutes."

"Do it now while I hitch up the trailer. That will give us ten minutes to say hello to each other as man and wife before we have to get out of here."

The romantic side to Cy sent ripples of delight through her nervous system. He was excitingly methodical. As soon as he left the trailer, she rushed to change clothes. Tonight she'd wear a new Western shirt with fringe and a new pair of jeans. She had to remember to remove the pearls and put in her gold cowboy-boot earrings.

Once she'd hung up her wedding suit and put on her Western outfit, she pulled on her cowboy boots. Then she put on her cowboy hat so she wouldn't forget it.

"Leave the hat off for a few minutes."

Her heart leaped when she realized Cy had already come back inside.

The burning in his eyes made her legs tremble.

"Come here to me, darling. I need to hold you for a few minutes so I can believe that you're really mine."

Like being underwater, she moved slowly toward him and slid her hands up his chest and around his neck. He lowered his head to kiss her mouth, and the world stood still. She couldn't get close enough. No kiss was long enough. They'd gone beyond words to a place where hearts and desires had taken over.

It seemed as if they'd barely had a moment together when she heard a rap on the trailer door. "Sorry to bother you, Kellie. I'm heading over to the arena. See you soon."

A sound of protest broke from Cy before he put her away from him. But he had to hold on to her so she wouldn't fall. "I shouldn't have started kissing you, Mrs. Vance."

"I'd have died if you hadn't, Mr. Vance."

December 1

"I've been nauseated for the last couple of days, Dr. Shay. I'm supposed to leave for the Finals championship in Las Vegas tomorrow, but I need something to help me get over this flu fast."

"You don't have the flu, Mrs. Vance. You're pregnant."

Kellie came close to fainting. "Are you positive?"

"Your blood test didn't lie."

"But I've been on birth control pills for over a year to regularize my periods."

"Even so, there are reasons why you weren't protected. Women who become pregnant while taking an oral contraceptive either miss one or more doses, or you take a dose at a different time from the normal interval. If you took one in the evening instead of the morning, that can throw things off."

She tried to think back. Had she done either of the things he'd just mentioned? Wait—the day of their marriage she might have taken the pill that night instead of that morning because she was so excited about meeting Cy. Maybe she did miss a dose or two. She simply couldn't remember.

But one thing was certain. Her obstetrician couldn't be wrong. She was going to have Cy's baby. The news filled her with a joy beyond comprehension. But her nausea was so severe, she couldn't possibly compete.

"I'll give you some sample packets of nausea pills. You can take something before bed and see how it affects you. For some women it works after a few days. With others, you just have to wait until the nausea passes with time."

"Thank you."

When she got into her car, she had to sit there for a few minutes before she felt she could drive home to the condo. Once she got there, she lay down on the couch and phoned Cy. She had to leave a message on his voice mail.

"Darling? Please call me ASAP. It's an emergency."

Half an hour later he came bounding through the back door of the kitchen. "Kellie?"

"I'm here on the couch."

He hurried into the living and knelt down by her. "You're pale. What's wrong?"

"I went to the doctor this afternoon. I thought I had the flu. Cy? We're going to have a baby. It had to have happened on our wedding night."

His eyes flared with a light she'd never seen before. "You're pregnant?"

"I know it doesn't seem possible, but the blood test didn't lie. Even though I'm so nauseated I want to die, I'm so happy to be carrying your baby, you just can't imagine."

He looked anxious and vulnerable. She'd never seen him like this before. "I'm so sorry you're feeling ill. What can I get you?"

"Some ice chips? I've taken one of the pills he gave me."

"Anything."

He was gone in a flash and brought some ice back in a cup. She put several chips on her tongue. "Will you phone the parents? We may need to postpone the wedding. Thank heaven the invitations haven't gone out yet."

Cy kissed her lips. "We'll send wedding announcements instead and wait until you're over your morning sickness before we have a reception."

"Will you call Olivia in Colorado Springs tonight? Tell her I have to withdraw from Finals because we're expecting. She'll take care of everything."

"Oh, Kellie—" He made a tortured sound in his throat. "To think my marrying you has caused you to miss the thing you've wanted most in life."

She shook her head. "You're wrong, my love. The first time we bumped into each other in Bandera, I knew I wanted you more than anything else in life. I've won lots of events over the years and have had my thrills. But knowing I'm going to have your baby is a gift beyond price."

"Darling!" Cy put his arms around her.

"I hope our parents will forgive us for getting married without telling them—" she spoke into his hair "—but to be honest, I feel so sick right now, I can't think about that."

"I'll take care of everything. You just lie here. Do you need a blanket?"

"No. The thought of heat makes me sicker. Oh—" she moaned. "You need to call Cody. Tell him he'll get his share of the money even though I didn't compete. I'll send him a check in a few days. They're getting married soon and will need it."

"I'll do it. What else?"

"Call TJ and ask him if he can spare you for twenty-four hours. I need you with me."

She could see his throat working. "As if I'd be anywhere else."

"Those psycho twins you took down changed the very structure of our lives. There should have been a happier, safer way to have met. But I wouldn't trade that week we spent together playing man and wife for anything on earth."

He smoothed the hair off her damp forehead. "I've said this before, but I'll say it again. I thought I'd died and gone to heaven."

"What a story we have to tell our baby one day." She closed her eyes, starting to feel sleepy. "I was the undercover bride of a Texas Ranger. Promise me something?"

"Anything, darling."

"If it's a girl, we're not naming her Sylvia."

While joyous laughter poured out of her husband, she reached for some more ice chips.

Men had it so easy. It wasn't fair. But she wouldn't have it any other way, and she wouldn't have any other man.

* * * * *

Watch for the next story in Rebecca Winters's
LONE STAR LAWMEN *miniseries,*
coming January 2016,
only from Harlequin American Romance!

REQUEST YOUR FREE BOOKS!
2 FREE NOVELS PLUS 2 FREE GIFTS!

HARLEQUIN®

American Romance®

LOVE, HOME & HAPPINESS

YES! Please send me 2 FREE Harlequin® American Romance® novels and my 2 FREE gifts (gifts are worth about $10). After receiving them, if I don't wish to receive any more books, I can return the shipping statement marked "cancel." If I don't cancel, I will receive 4 brand-new novels every month and be billed just $4.74 per book in the U.S. or $5.49 per book in Canada. That's a savings of at least 12% off the cover price! It's quite a bargain! Shipping and handling is just 50¢ per book in the U.S. and 75¢ per book in Canada.* I understand that accepting the 2 free books and gifts places me under no obligation to buy anything. I can always return a shipment and cancel at any time. Even if I never buy another book, the two free books and gifts are mine to keep forever.

154/354 HDN GHZZ

Name	(PLEASE PRINT)	

Address		Apt. #

City	State/Prov.	Zip/Postal Code

Signature (if under 18, a parent or guardian must sign)

Mail to the **Reader Service:**
IN U.S.A.: P.O. Box 1867, Buffalo, NY 14240-1867
IN CANADA: P.O. Box 609, Fort Erie, Ontario L2A 5X3

Want to try two free books from another line?
Call 1-800-873-8635 or visit www.ReaderService.com.

* Terms and prices subject to change without notice. Prices do not include applicable taxes. Sales tax applicable in N.Y. Canadian residents will be charged applicable taxes. Offer not valid in Quebec. This offer is limited to one order per household. Not valid for current subscribers to Harlequin American Romance books. All orders subject to credit approval. Credit or debit balances in a customer's account(s) may be offset by any other outstanding balance owed by or to the customer. Please allow 4 to 6 weeks for delivery. Offer available while quantities last.

Your Privacy—The Reader Service is committed to protecting your privacy. Our Privacy Policy is available online at www.ReaderService.com or upon request from the Reader Service.

We make a portion of our mailing list available to reputable third parties that offer products we believe may interest you. If you prefer that we not exchange your name with third parties, or if you wish to clarify or modify your communication preferences, please visit us at www.ReaderService.com/consumerschoice or write to us at Reader Service Preference Service, P.O. Box 9062, Buffalo, NY 14240-9062. Include your complete name and address.

*Doctors Gavin Monroe and Violet McCabe
have just been named co-guardians of an orphaned
baby girl and need to work together to find the child
a permanent home...*

Read on for a sneak peak of
LONE STAR BABY, *from* Cathy Gillen Thacker's
McCABE MULTIPLES *miniseries.*

The usual idealism shining in her pretty brown eyes, Violet turned to Gavin, frowned and said, "Obviously we can't adopt baby Ava together." She walked back outside and he followed her. "We barely know each other."

Barely?

While it was true they hadn't hung out together as kids and had run in different social circles—it was certainly different now that they were both physicians.

Irked to find her so quick to discount the time they *had* spent together, Gavin stepped in once again to lend a hand unpacking the trailer, pointing out, "We've worked together for the past five years while we completed our residencies and fellowship training."

"You know what I mean. Yes, I know your preferred ways of dealing with certain medical situations, just as you surely know mine. But when it comes to the intricate personal details of your life, I don't know you any better than I know the rest of the staff at the hospital." Violet plucked a lamp base out of the pile of belongings, rooting around until she found the shade. "And you don't really know me at all, either."

Gavin's jaw tightened. Oh, he knew her, all right. Maybe better than she thought.

For instance he knew her preferred coffee was a skinny vanilla latte. And that she loved enchiladas above all else—to the point she'd sampled all twenty-five types from the local Tex-Mex restaurant.

He tore his gaze from the barest hint of cleavage in the V of her T-shirt and concentrated instead on the dismayed hint of color sweeping her delicate cheeks.

"And whose fault is that?" he inquired.

"Mine, obviously," she said with a temperamental lift of her finely arched brow, "since I prefer to keep a firewall between my professional and private lives."

More like a nuclear shield, he thought grimly.

Don't miss
LONE STAR BABY
by Cathy Gillen Thacker,
available September 2015 everywhere
Harlequin® American Romance®
books and ebooks are sold.

www.Harlequin.com

Love the Harlequin book you just read?

Your opinion matters.

Review this book on your favorite
book site, review site, blog or your own
social media properties and share
your opinion with other readers!

HARLEQUIN®

A *Romance* FOR EVERY MOOD™

JUST CAN'T GET ENOUGH?

Join our social communities
and talk to us online.

You will have access to the latest
news on upcoming titles and special
promotions, but most importantly,
you can talk to other fans about your
favorite Harlequin reads.

Harlequin.com/Community

 Facebook.com/HarlequinBooks

 Twitter.com/HarlequinBooks

Pinterest.com/HarlequinBooks